COLLISION

Part One of the Colliding Worlds Trilogy

RACHEL AUKES

WAYPOINT BOOKS

WAYPOINT BOOKS

COLLISION

Waypoint Books LLC

Cover Design by Evernight Designs

Edited by Kriegler Editing Services and Terri King Editing Service

Chapter One

Ouachita Forest, Arkansas

I t wasn't the first time a good idea had come back to bite Sienna Wolfe in the ass, but it could be the last. She checked her phone again. *No signal*. She shoved the phone back into her pocket. Taking a deep breath of autumn air laced with the scent of burning wires, she clicked on the flashlight and stepped into the wingless aircraft.

The light sliced through the smoky blackness and fell upon a figure slumped over the instrument panel. The pilot's dark flight suit and mask covered him from head to toe, making it impossible to tell if he was still alive or not.

Trembling with adrenaline, she stepped closer and held her left palm an inch from his covered face. Warm shallow breaths tickled her skin. The breath she'd been holding rushed from her lungs in a frosty puff of relief.

He's alive.

She ran her hands over his body, feeling for broken bones or fabric wet with blood. Finding neither, she looked for a way to remove the face mask that seemed to be a part of his flight suit. A persistent beep echoed through the cylindrical ship, which she tried to ignore. Inching back to full height, Sienna paused, thinking through her next steps.

Plane crashes in the Arkansas forests were often fatal. Even though she had a pilot's license, she'd never been around a plane crash, let alone in one. When she'd heard the telltale sound of trees breaking not far from her cabin, she'd jumped onto her ATV to investigate. It hadn't taken long to discover the smoke and locate the ship.

Sienna figured it had to be military, given how unusual it was. So super-secret, the ship didn't even have an N-number. Adding that fact to a middle-of-the-night, low-level flight meant the military was likely testing some new addition to their fleet. She was surprised—and disappointed—to not see rescue helicopters already, leaving her as the sole first responder.

She blew out a breath and rubbed her hands together. "I can do this."

While checking the pilot for injuries one more time before attempting to move him, a small sound under the louder beeping distracted her. Shining the beam toward the rhythmic *plip-plop*, the light fell on rivulets flowing down the wall toward a crumpled mass of sparking instrument panel. Bending down on one knee, she dipped a finger in the liquid and smelled the clear, almost gel-like substance. It was foreign, like an exotic nighttime plant, but the underlying hint of kerosene was unmistakable; it had to be some sort of jet fuel.

It was then that the sound clicked something in her brain. The beeps were speeding up; what used to be a second pause between each was now half that. She'd assumed the beeps were a proximity alarm.

Her lips parted. *Oh, hell.*

It made perfect sense that the military would have an

auto-destruct on new technology to keep it from falling into the wrong hands. In a rush, Sienna fidgeted with seamless seatbelts that had no visible latches. Her fingers brushed over a switch that moved. She heard a snap, and in a blur, the belts retracted into the floor. As the pilot crumpled forward, she slid her hands under his arms to keep his head from hitting the floor.

At the risk of further injury, she dragged the man toward the door. His rubber-soled boots dragged across the floor, the friction pushing the limits of her strength. Her hands slipped, and the pilot fell with a *thud*.

She bent over to get hold of him again but stopped cold when movement caught her eye. The trail of fuel had now become a river and was running down toward a section of smoking wires. Her eyes widened. Interlacing her fingers around the man's chest in a Heimlich-maneuver style hold, she put everything she had into hefting him through the doorway and outside the ship.

Her arms burned as she dragged him across the ground. Not knowing how far away she needed to be, she kept dragging him. Her legs shook. Her back felt like it could give out at any moment.

"What do you think you're doing?"

Startled, she dropped the pilot and snapped around to find another man nearly hidden by the trees. Relief flooded her at no longer being alone. "Oh, thank God you're here. Help, please. He's hurt bad. We've got to get clear. I think the ship could blow."

He made no move.

She'd heard about that type of response dozens of times before. How onlookers froze at the sight of an accident. Just her luck she got one of those. Her jaw tightened. "Hey, you. I need your help here."

He stepped forward then. Tall as a professional wrestler,

he wore a strange soldier-meets-gladiator outfit. His silver hair glistened in the moonlight. But what most drew her attention were the flesh-like, tattoo-covered wings that spanned behind him. Strange, since it was nowhere close to Halloween.

She shook it off. "Do you have a car nearby? Otherwise, we can get him onto my ATV—Hey!"

He grabbed her wrist and yanked her to him. Pinning her arms against her, he patted her pockets down with his free hand.

Fear brought forth a fresh surge of adrenaline. She bucked and kicked at him. "What are you doing? Let go!"

He ignored her and pulled out her phone then sent her tumbling to the ground. He dropped the phone, pulled out a gun, and fired. The blast, strangely quiet, obliterated her phone with the same results as a large caliber. Sienna froze.

He holstered his weapon. "You need to come with me. You've seen things you should never have seen."

Sienna clawed against his iron grip, but he pulled her in the direction away from her cabin, her struggles not hampering his stride in the least.

"No!" she yelled and grabbed a tree not much larger than a sapling. She held on tight. The small branches sliced her palm as she was pulled away. A blast of heat shot past her, and the grip on her wrist loosened. She rolled onto her knees and looked up to see her assailant lying on the ground, smoke rising from a gaping chest wound. She jerked her attention back to the pilot, who was now conscious, leaning against a tree a few feet away, and shakily holding a weapon pointed in her direction.

She held up both hands. "Please, don't shoot. I'm unarmed. I'm here to help."

She couldn't see his expression, what with his face being covered, but he lowered the gun and she let out a sigh of relief. Keeping an eye on the pilot, she gingerly leaned over the newcomer to check for a pulse. Not that she needed to; a hole had burned straight through his chest. The guy never had a chance.

Her finger brushed against a wing as she leaned back on her heels, and she jerked her hand away from the unexpected warmth emanating from the flesh-like prop.

Coming to her feet, she focused on her breathing. "He's dead."

The face mask, as before, blocked any expression.

She kept her hands where he could see them. "Your ship has a fuel leak. I think your ship is going to blow."

"Are you aligned with the Draeken?" he asked.

Draeken. That name rang a bell; something her mother had said a couple months back. Sienna shook away the thought, making a mental note to ask Kat about it later. "I don't know what you're talking about."

He lifted the gun again, directly at her heart.

Sienna didn't think, or realize what she was doing, as she swung her leg out and kicked the pilot in the head. The weapon flew from his hand. She dived for the gun, fumbling through the leaves to grab it. Standing above the pilot, she gripped the weapon with both hands and aimed it at his chest. Waited a moment. Nudged him with her toe. Waited another moment. Nudged him again.

In the distance, she could still hear the beeps, only now they were even closer together.

Leave him.

That was the logical thing to do. After all, the pilot had just killed a man and had been going to shoot her. But leaving someone to bleed out in an Arkansas forest went against everything Sienna stood for.

Tucking the weapon into the waistband of her cargos, she managed to hoist the pilot onto the back of the ATV she'd ridden in on. His legs dangled over the sides of the rack. She then leapt onto the seat in front of him and gunned the throttle. The engine roared, tires kicking up dirt and pine needles.

A massive boom rocked the ground and a shockwave nearly sent her tumbling from the ATV. Then, as if she was a sliver of metal drawn to a magnet, heat sucked her back toward the explosion. There was no air to breathe, let alone scream. She hunkered down over the handlebars with a death-grip and pushed the throttle in all the way, holding on for dear life. The ATV chewed its way forward inch by inch through the ravenous suction.

Then, as suddenly as it came, the wind vanished and the woods hushed, like someone had hit the mute button. Slowing the ATV, she looked over her shoulder then slammed the brakes. She hopped off and stood, staring blankly at the crash site.

Confusion settled over her. There was no fire. No debris. No sign of wreckage. It was as though nothing had been there, like the ship and the shredded trees around it had imploded into nothingness.

Aside from the eerie absence of nighttime forest noises, everything appeared normal. Nothing to even hint that a ship had crashed there less than an hour earlier.

"Impossible," she whispered.

Sienna didn't know how long she stood there in open-mouthed shock. Regular glances back at her still-present passenger proved that everything had been real and not some hallucination. Her heart felt like it was pumping lead, making it difficult to catch her breath. Without her phone, her only option was to head back to her place and contact the authorities.

The half-mile drive through the winding pine woods felt interminable. She clutched the handlebars in a vice-grip as she tore around trees, ignoring small branches whipping at her face. She slowed only to glance back every once in a while at her unconscious passenger.

When she finally pulled up to the front steps of her stone cabin, adrenaline still surged through her veins. She knew the sensation all too well. As a humanitarian relief worker, she'd been in the middle of a half dozen civil conflicts in as many Third World countries. But she'd never, ever looked down the barrel of a gun before. It was a feeling she hoped to never experience again.

What made things worse was that the dead man had destroyed her only working phone, as the cabin had no landline.

Willing herself into action with a grunt, she dragged the pilot off the ATV and up the stone steps, the smooth material of his flight suit making her job all the harder to maintain her grip. Seconds felt like minutes as she hauled the dead weight into her home and dropped him unceremoniously on her couch. Her muscles shook with fatigue. Sweat ran down her temple and tickled her cheek.

She pulled out the gun with one hand as she swept back hair that had become plastered to her face. She stared blankly at the black weapon for only a second before she rushed into her bedroom, removed the Glock she stored in her night-stand, and checked to make sure it was still loaded with one round in the barrel. Its heft and familiarity comforted her, helping her to calm down. She then hid the pilot's weapon deep in her closet.

Eying her clothes, she yanked out a couple flannel shirts, gave the fabric a quick tug, and hurried back to living room. There, she tied his wrists together with one shirt then used the second shirt to bind his wrists over his head and to the floor lamp. She knew it wouldn't hold him for more than a second if he tried to attack, but a second could make the difference between Sienna becoming a victim or firing her gun.

Finished, her stomach churned as she leveled her handgun on him. When he didn't move, she pulled out the chair at the computer desk across the room from the couch. She may not have a land line phone, but she did have high-speed Internet. After a quick search, she pulled up the Hot Springs emergency services website. She opened a chat message and entered minimal details about the crash, the pilot, and her address.

She looked back at the pilot. She hoped someone would be monitoring the messages, or else she'd be forced into driving the man to the hospital an hour away. The idea of negotiating winding roads with one eye and a gun leveled on her passenger sounded less than ideal.

While she waited for a return message, she searched the internet for "Draeken" but the search results yielded nothing. She then typed a quick email to her mother:

Hey Kat—Hope you're enjoying Argentina. Need info on that "Draeken" thing you mentioned last month. It's important. Love, Sienna

Sienna wished she'd listened to her mother more closely. She leaned back in the chair and kept the gun level on her 'guest' as she waited for a response. Seconds passed like hours, and she found herself tapping her feet as she waited.

Still no response from either the emergency services or from the pilot.

After waiting a full minute without him showing any sign of consciousness, she headed to the bathroom and grabbed anything that could be used as a medical supply.

She knew he could die without medical attention. Her legs didn't want to move, but she willed them forward, edging closer and closer until she reached him and dropped the supplies into a pile on the floor.

She was no medic, but she knew the first rule in any accident was to stabilize the patient. She couldn't just sit around and wait while he died.

His breathing was steady, although not strong by any means. He likely had internal injuries. She felt around his neck for the edge of his mask. Locating it, ever so carefully she rolled it up then yanked it off.

And gasped.

His skin looked like he'd taken a shower in liquid gold. Dark tribal-style tattoos swirled over his skin, but there didn't seem to be a specific design to the way they curved around his neck and onto his face—a face with a nasty bruise forming around an even nastier swollen eye that was no doubt caused by her boot. She winced at the harm she'd caused, but then reminded herself that he'd been the aggressor, not her.

She leaned back.

Holy. Shit. First, the guy with wings; now this.

Tattoos were one thing, but this was something else. Even if they were some kind of military thing, there seemed no logical reason for the anti-stealth glimmer that covered his skin.

No way was this guy real. Despite a successful career in selling the possibility of it, she'd never really believed in it. There was no such thing as an… she could barely even think the word.

Alien.

Chapter Two

S ienna half-expected to see a cameraman pop out and yell "Surprise!", but no one did, which meant she was alone with someone who was like no one she'd seen before. She had assumed the pilot was military, but it was far more likely that both men were members of some rival cultish gangs.

She was in way over her head—and she'd seen plenty of crazy in her life. For her first eighteen years, she'd followed her parents across the globe with their humanitarian efforts. After a relatively normal college career, she spent the next fifteen years consulting with the military.

But this guy…

And the other guy…

A shiver ran across her skin as fear seeped into her. If only she had her phone, she could call 9-1-1. Instead, the mess fell squarely on Sienna's shoulders until someone checked the chat message she'd left. For better or worse, she was the one who'd witnessed the crash.

She stood over the man for another long moment. Convinced he wasn't playing possum, she set her gun down and checked for injuries. She was more careful and slow this time as she ran her hands over his arms, feeling for broken bones. She then moved to his chest and down his abdomen, stopping when she discovered a spot where the material was saturated.

She tried to cut down the front of the flight suit, but the thin fabric was stronger than she would have guessed. Even with both hands clasping the shears, cutting through the fabric was a painfully slow process. When the final bit of fabric covering his torso was cut away, she found the source of the wetness about an inch below his rib cage. Blood seeped from a deep gouge, but it was unlike any blood she'd ever seen before. It was thick and dark and definitely not crimson.

In a shocked daze, Sienna closed her mouth and watched his chest, covered in tattoos and small X-shaped scars, rise and fall and rise again, the wound continuing to ooze the strange fluid. This was something her unerring sense of logic couldn't defend. Here she was, watching dark liquid gold bleed from a wound. The color was so *alien*.

When the pilot still showed no signs of consciousness, Sienna leaned in to get a better look at the nasty gouge. Grabbing a bottle of antiseptic and some cotton swabs, she dabbed the liquid across his skin. New blood rose with every gentle touch she made. The cut was too deep for a bandage, and too much for her meager first-aid skills. Even if she was successful in stopping the bleeding, infection was another story.

She glanced back at her computer; still no response to her chat message.

Grimacing, she threaded a needle and placed her palm on his chest near the wound. The instant before she pierced the skin, heat bloomed under her hand. She jolted back and dropped the needle.

She looked at her hand, but it looked normal. She looked

at his wound. Where her hand had been, his skin shimmered more brightly. Fresh, scarred skin now covered the edges of the wound. Her jaw slackened.

Searching the floor, she located the needle and plunked it onto the coffee table. Rubbing her neck, Sienna tried to make sense out of what had happened. Maybe it was shock, maybe it was the after-effect of adrenaline wearing off, but she made only a half-hearted attempt to reason with herself before gingerly placing her palm against his skin again.

After a moment, heat hit her hand. She sat on the edge of the coffee table, feeling slightly woozy, but didn't remove her hand as she watched fresh scar tissue form over the bloody cut. All the while, heat tickled her palm as though her hand rested on an anthill. When a fresh scar filled in where the bloody gouge had been, the tickling disappeared, and she pulled her hand away.

Lightheaded from the surreal experience, she leaned back, stared at her patient, and found eyes darker than midnight, without any surrounding white, watching her, squinting in the light.

In a flash she was off the table and standing several feet away, Glock leveled at him. "Who are you?"

"Turn down the light. It hurts my eyes," he said. He tugged at his restraints while he muttered strange, lyrical words that, judging by the look on his face, were more likely a string of cuss words.

"No," she answered. "Not until you answer my question."

He stilled. "I am Legian. I mean no harm to you."

"Then why did you point your gun at me?"

"I thought you may have been aligned with the other one."

"Who was he?"

"A murderer."

She swallowed, not knowing which man had been the

greater danger, if not both. She did not lower her gun, but she did walk over and dim the lights. "I'm Sienna. Welcome to my home."

"Why am I here?"

"You were hurt, and I couldn't leave you at your ship. It blew up."

After a moment, the pilot began tugging at his restraints again, showing no surprise at the fact that his ship had been destroyed.

Sienna frowned. "Did you expect to die back there?"

At those words, he looked down from his restraints and met her eyes with a look of resolve.

She narrowed an eye at the pilot. "Why are you here?"

He didn't answer for the longest time. Instead, he lay there. "Release me," was all he said.

A soft snort escaped her. "Like hell. You were going to shoot me."

He yanked against his restraints and grunted before surrendering to the couch with a wince. It was then she saw a pool of blood she'd completely missed before.

"You're still bleeding."

"Release me."

"No way." She took tentative steps closer, all the while keeping the gun securely aimed at him. She shot a hard gaze at him. "I can try to help, but I *will* shoot you if you try anything."

He watched her with a clenched jaw for a moment before giving a tight nod.

With his wrists tied, she couldn't roll him all the way onto his stomach. Unable to see and stuck using only one hand, she had to work with touch alone, feeling for the wound. She moved her fingers over his skin until he sucked in a breath. Thick, warm moisture enveloped her fingers near his spine.

"Ow!" Sienna snapped back her finger to find a bead of crimson blood forming on the tip.

If he'd been a *normal* person, she'd leave the shrapnel in there until it could be removed by a professional, but this man was anything but normal. She softened her gaze. "There's something still in there. My guess is that you can't do your healing thing with it in there. I'll pull it out on the count of three."

"Three what?"

"Never mind." She gripped the metal, and it came out with a quick tug. He grunted but didn't yank away. She pulled back and tossed the shard onto the coffee table. It made a metallic ping when it bounced off the hard oak.

Fresh blood began spilling out. Watching him watching her, she flattened her hand on his back. Just like the first time, heat surged. A familiar blanket of dizziness fell over her, and she fought to keep the gun steady. After several more seconds, the bleeding slowed, and then stopped altogether.

Exhausted, she shakily held the gun trained on him as she took a seat on the table, using her knee to steady her aim.

His brows furrowed. "You helped me. Why did you not break contact?"

"You were hurt. Touching you seemed to help." She paused. "How do you do that?"

"My people can use energy to heal." He examined Sienna from his prone position. "Release me. Please." He gritted out the words through clenched teeth, making them sound more like an ultimatum than a request.

She shook her head. "Not until help gets here."

Suddenly, he lunged forward. His hands pulled free from the restraints faster than she'd thought possible.

He knocked her to the floor, and her head banged back against the hardwood. Her vision tunneled, and the gun was yanked from her hand. Still, she managed to kick and punch him like a rabid wolverine. Not that it did any good. When the room quit swimming, her arms were pinned and his face was inches from hers, his warm breath tickling her lips.

She hit him with the only thing she could still move, her forehead. Stars danced across her vision, and shards of pain ran through her brain. He grimaced, but never even flinched. Still pinned as tightly as ever, all she could do now was glare. "Let me go."

He frowned. "Why did you help me?" he asked, deflecting her command.

In response, she struggled harder, and his grip tightened. "Ow, ow, ow," she muttered. He loosened his grip just enough so that she didn't feel like her bones would be pulverized.

"Why did you help me?" he repeated.

With a drawn-out sigh, Sienna laid her head back on the floor. He had her, and he knew it. "I'm not going to leave someone to die." She glared. "No matter how much of an asshole they are."

He watched her for a moment then the weight lifted from her and he released her wrists. She pulled them to her chest, rubbing circulation back into them, before she sat up.

She jumped when she saw a second man, dressed head to toe in the same type of suit the pilot was dressed in, standing next to Legian. This man was holding the same kind of weapon Legian had used to kill the Draeken, and it was pointed directly at her.

The two men began speaking in their strange language, seemingly ignoring Sienna, yet the gun never wavered in the newcomer's grip. She thought about making a move to grab her Glock, which was now sitting on a side table, but thought better of the plan since Legian stood only a foot away from that table. As the men conversed, the only word she could make out was *Draeken*, though she figured much of the conversation revolved around her—or more aptly, what to do with her.

Her breathing was hard and tight until the newcomer holstered his gun, and she felt some relief.

Legian stepped forward and held out a hand to help her stand. She slapped it away and pushed herself shakily to her feet.

"This is Bente," Legian said. "He will bring us back to our base."

Her gaze narrowed. "Us?"

"You must come with us. We cannot risk our presence to be known," Legian replied.

She held up her hands. "I won't say anything. You have my word. I swear," she said, her voice pleading.

"We can't take any risks," Bente replied. "You either come with us or you die."

Legian scowled. "Bente."

Fear built within her like a mouse stepping into a trap. She looked at the doorway then to the window, wondering if she could escape in time.

"You cannot stay here. It isn't safe," Legian continued. "I give you my word, you will not be harmed. You saved my life, and I will protect yours."

She didn't believe him for a second. The newcomer had already made it quite clear what would happen to her if she tried to run. She took a deep breath before looking up into dark eyes that contained no white. Goose bumps flitted across her skin. She lifted her chin. "Let's go."

Chapter Three

L egian didn't bother blindfolding Sienna, since she couldn't have seen much anyway; the inside of the windowless ship was as dark as the nighttime forest outside. Legian had buckled her into a seat behind the cockpit, and now sat across from her. She could just make out his shape, and had no doubt he watched her the entire trip to their base.

The ship flew differently than the planes she'd piloted. Small aircraft needed runaways and momentum to build lift, while this ship lifted from the ground like a Harrier but was far quieter and smoother. She wanted to view the cockpit, to see if the controls and instruments where similar to what she was familiar with. After all, the laws of gravity and aerodynamics were universal.

The ship landed ten minutes or so after takeoff. The short flight surprised her, and she wondered if their base was close to her cabin, or if the ship just flew incredibly fast. Probably a bit of both.

Bente opened the door and stepped out into the dim light filtering in through the space.

"It will be a moment," Legian said as he unbuckled the straps on her seat. "Bente needs to update our *tahcaya*."

She pushed to her feet and took a step to the door.

"You have my word that you will be safe," he said.

Unconvinced, she said nothing. Instead, she listened to the sound of voices trickling into the ship. She tried to make out the words, but it was all in the alien language she'd heard Legian and Bente speaking back at her cabin.

After what seemed like minutes, Bente popped his head back into the ship and looked at Sienna. "Come."

With Bente in front of her and Legian behind, she felt like a prisoner even though she wore no restraints. As she stepped out of the ship, she found herself in a large enclosed hangar. The lights were dim here as well, and she'd wished they were a bit brighter so that she could make out more details.

Bente stopped and stepped to her side while Legian stepped to her other side. They were at the edge of the hangar. Dozens of ships like the one they'd arrived in were parked around the walls, draped in shadows, while several larger ships occupied the center.

Before her stood a male in a plain black uniform with no insignia, even though he bore the air of a leader. He was tall like Legian and Bente, but his hair was longer and tattoos covered much of his visible skin; one in particular vined around his eye and gave him the look of a pirate. Several more aliens—some male, some female—stood behind him. All had golden skin and pure black eyes, and wore the simple black uniform.

Legian spoke in the alien language, and this time she clearly heard her name among the words. When Legian finished, he turned to her. "Sienna, this is Apolo, our *tahcaya* —our leader."

The man stepped closer, and she girded herself to not take a step back.

"Hello, Sienna. You may call me Apolo." His English was near-perfect. "I lead the Sephian forces on this small planet. And, as you have helped one of my own, you have the privilege of being the first of your race to meet with me. However, your appearance has raised a complication that I'd hoped not to deal with so soon. As such, now I must decide what to do with you."

You mean you have to decide whether to kill me or let me live, she thought to herself, but said nothing.

Apolo gestured to the people behind him. "You must understand, there are lives on this base dependent on secrecy."

"Apolo," Legian said. "Sienna saved my life, and I have pledged her safety here. She accompanied us without coercion. I believe she means us no harm."

Sienna practically chortled. 'Without coercion' was a stretch.

Apolo gave Legian a surprised look and turned to Bente. "Is this true? He has already made a pledge?"

Bente nodded. "Yes. Trust me, I thought the same thing when I heard it."

Apolo thought for a moment. "Well, then, it is settled. Legian, Sienna is your responsibility. Do you understand?"

"Yes," Legian said without hesitation.

"Good," Apolo said, and turned to Sienna. "You will be welcomed as a guest here. In return, I request that you meet with me to help me learn more about your people and culture. You will not be harmed unless you intend harm to any of my people. Can you meet these expectations?"

As he spoke the words, she knew that what she was hearing was an ultimatum. Her second one tonight. Essentially, he'd just told her 'Do everything I say and you get to live for now'. Frustration roiled through her at the unfairness of the situation. She hadn't asked for any of this. Her entire life had just been taken from her because she'd been in the wrong place at the wrong time. She looked at Apolo, tamping down any emotion that may show in her features, and said simply, "I accept your conditions."

His gaze narrowed as though he could see through her façade. Then he smiled. "Good. We will speak in an hour. I advise you to use the time to bathe. You have blood and dirt on you. Bente will gather some of your belongings when he ensures your home is cleaned of our presence."

He turned and left with most of his entourage, while Bente and two others headed back to the ship.

Chills raced over her skin at the thought of strangers rifling through her things. She spun around to see Bente disappear into the ship, and was overwhelmed with an urge to follow him even though she knew she could never go home; not with their permission anyway.

"Come with me," Legian said. "I will show you to your room."

She stood a little taller as she turned toward Legian then fell in alongside him as they walked through the hangar and down several hallways. With the lights down so low, it felt like she was walking through a large building with only nightlights on. Every door they passed was closed, giving her no inkling as to a possible exit. Each door had a small touchpad set in the wall next to it which she suspected needed a badge of some kind to open them. Her hopes fell more and more as she realized this place made for the perfect prison.

Legian turned, and she stumbled into him. She grunted. "Sorry. It's hard to see in here."

"Oh," he said. "I hadn't thought of that. On my world, my people are accustomed to moving about in the dark. Our days and nights are opposite to humans' cycles. We sleep during the light hours and are active during the dark. I will get you glasses to help you see."

He stopped at a door and tapped on the pad, as though playing the beat of some tune she didn't recognize. The door opened, and he gestured inside. "This is your room."

The lights came on at the same dim level as the hallways. Legian spoke. "Lights, increase twenty percent." The room lit up enough for Sienna to see, but caused Legian to squint.

She stepped over the threshold. The room was sparsely furnished with a bed, couch, what looked like a bar, and a door to what she hoped was a human-like bathroom. As she looked over the weapons hung on the wall, the unmade bed, and the drinks at the bar, she froze. It took a deep breath before she could swallow her fear enough to speak. "Someone lives here already."

"It is my room," he said. "You stay with me now."

Her jaw slackened. She spun to face him. "What is the meaning of this?"

"I am sorry. We have no free residences, and even if we did—"

"I couldn't have one," she interrupted. "Because I am a prisoner."

"If you were a prisoner, you'd be in a holding cell."

"I'd rather be in a holding cell than sharing a bed with you!"

He took a step back and held his hands out as though surrendering. "I am sorry for the situation you've found your-self in. I have given you my word. I will not harm you, and I mean that in all ways, but this room is the only option for you at this time. I claimed you as my responsibility, which means I am responsible for your life, wellbeing, and behavior at all times. Perhaps, once Apolo allows it, we can make new arrangements. Until then, you will sleep on the bed. I will sleep on the sofa."

She stared at him for a lengthy moment. She had no control, and she wanted to scream. "Fine." She sighed and scanned the room. "Where do I get cleaned up?"

He led her to the bathroom. "Bente will return shortly with clean clothes. Until then, you can wear your current clothes or I can find you something else."

"I'll wear my clothes," she said quickly.

After he showed her how to use the shower, he left her alone, though she wondered if she was being watched even then. It was one thing being imprisoned, but an entirely different thing to have an alien jailer a few feet away in the same room. She showered, changed, and left the bathroom to find Legian gone as well as the weapons on the wall. She spent the next several minutes pacing the room, handling every item she found to see if anything could be used as a weapon or aid in her escape.

By the time Legian returned with a snack that tasted much like a protein bar, she'd scoured the small room, finding nothing that she could use. He then delivered her to Apolo. Apolo's questioning wasn't nearly as painful as Sienna had expected. The medical examination, on the other hand, was far worse. She'd chortled when she'd first seen the table full of probe-like instruments laid out when she entered, making it look like a scene from a B-grade sci-fi movie.

Lucky for her, those instruments were just parts for a faulty wall panel being repaired. Unlucky for her, the scanner the doctor used wasn't calibrated for human physiology, and she ended up with second-degree burns over much of her back. The base's primary doctor, Fayel, whom she called Doc, had the disposition of many doctors she'd met in her life.

Apologetic for the harm he'd caused, he'd used salves to ease her burns, and she found it easy to not fear him.

She'd been given the day to recuperate, since that was when the Sephians rested. Exhausted, she fell asleep. It helped that Legian didn't snore to remind her that she wasn't alone in the room. Even so, she shot awake often as memories mixed with unfamiliar surroundings to create new and horrible dreams.

She had lain awake in bed for a couple hours before Legian woke and got ready for the night. Before he left, a Sephian female arrived.

"Hello, Sienna. I'm Nalea. I'm here to give you a tour of the base," she said. She could have been a double for a young Sigourney Weaver; almost a double, but not quite. Nalea sported glittery skin, pure ebony eyes, and long pitch-black hair.

They stepped into the dim hallway, and Nalea handed her a pair of sunglasses. "Here, these Draeken *tensatlen* will help you see."

Sienna slid them on. Immediately, the hallway lightened to where she could see all the details. She did a three-sixty, taking in everything. She lowered the glasses for a moment before pushing them back up her nose. "Wow. Sunglasses that *brighten* everything."

Sienna walked alongside Nalea through the long hallway, noticing screens on the walls and touchpads at every door. "This base isn't really a base," she said. "It's simply our ship. That's why the doors and walls may seem overbuilt."

"It's huge," Sienna said.

Nalea shrugged. "It's the largest Sephian ship, but it's tiny compared to a Draeken core ship."

As they continued their tour, Sienna noticed Nalea watching her. "What?" Sienna asked.

"Have you figured out any escape routes yet?"

Sienna became rigid. "What are you talking about?"

Nalea rolled her eyes. "I'd be doing the same if I was in your shoes. I saw you checking out every nick and cranny."

"Nook and cranny," Sienna said.

"What?"

"You said it wrong. It's 'nook and cranny'. Nick is a guy's name."

"Oh," Nalea said. "I don't blame you for looking for ways out. But even though you can't leave, you aren't a prisoner."

Sienna's brows rose. "Being held against my will is the exact definition of 'prisoner'."

"Or 'slave'," Nalea said. "That's why we came to your planet. Let me tell you about the Noble War to end slavery and how we drove the Draeken from Sephia…"

Nalea spent the rest of the walking tour telling Sienna the history of the Sephians and the Draeken, and why both had ended up on Earth.

The tour ended at a large circular room lined with tables. "This is the Commons," Nalea said. "It's the only room, other than the hangar, large enough to hold everyone at once. We eat here and have ship-wide meetings here. It's the heart of the vessel. As you can see, all hallways merge here." She motioned to the hub-and-spoke architecture before turning back to Sienna. "You must be hungry. Let me show you how to get food and drink."

Nalea led Sienna through the food line, which was incredibly similar to how a school cafeteria would work, except the food here was made to order. The cook spoke English, but Sienna recognized none of the dishes—all looked like brown mush. Nalea ordered for Sienna. "*Mulhean* is our most popular dish. I think you'll like it."

Sienna and Nalea sat at a table near one of the hallway entrances. Sienna's stomach growled. With the exception of a couple protein-like bars Legian had given her in the morning, it'd been a full day since she'd eaten.

Nalea dug in. Sienna took a big bite of the paste. It had a mashed consistency with crunchy, crystalline *something* to add texture. The only flavor she could glean was akin to Lima beans. She slowed her chewing.

"Do you like it?" Nalea asked.

Sienna forced herself to swallow. "It's… interesting. A bit bland. Do you have any salt?"

Nalea shook her head and frowned. "No. This is our most flavorful dish. Want me to get you something else?"

Sienna shook her head. "No. This is fine." She forced down the rest of the meal and drank a full glass of water. At least the water tasted normal.

As Nalea talked, Sienna found herself entranced by the woman's tattoos, which were lighter than those she'd seen on Legian, Bente, and Apolo. Nalea glanced at her hands and back up at Sienna. "Ah, my *soullare* intrigues you."

"*Soullare?* Is that what you call your tattoos?" Sienna asked.

Nalea smiled. "*Soullare* is not a tattoo. We are born with it. They say it was camouflage for our ancestors, but all Sephians still have it, though for some reason it's far darker on men. Our *soullare* is unique to each of us and is a source of pride." She wagged a brow. "And, it can be very sexy."

Sienna grinned as she took another bite. Talking with Nalea was easy, as though they were friends. She began to wonder if the Sephians weren't so different from humans or if she was developing Stockholm Syndrome.

As the days passed, Sienna looked for exits less and, instead, sought opportunities to learn more about the Sephians and how she could help stop the Draeken from enslaving humans.

By the third week, her body had adjusted to Sephian food,

and she finally felt at full strength in the opposite circadian schedule.

She had also picked up on the now-familiar scent every Sephian naturally carried. It had taken a week before she noticed the base smelled like a faint, soft rain. Now she couldn't imagine how she hadn't noticed it right away.

She also no longer feared Legian, although she still didn't know what to make of him. He had an aggressive personality and often bossed her around, telling her what to do and where to go, but as soon as she snapped back, he'd back down and become a puppy. She hadn't seen him do that around others, and wondered if he feared her because she was human.

Then, one evening, she walked into the bathroom, not realizing he was in there. She plowed right into his bare chest as he stepped out of the shower.

"Sorr—" she began, but the word melted away as she took in his nakedness.

He stood there. "When you look at me like that, I want to —you shouldn't look at me like that."

She looked up to find him watching her intently. In a rush, she spun around, closed the door, grabbed a drink, and sat on the edge of the bed, looking away from the bathroom. It had been over three years since her husband, Bobby, was killed by a driver too busy texting her BFF. Three years since she left the city life behind and moved away from humanity, away from senselessness. And three long years since she thought about touching a man. She reminded herself that Legian wasn't really a man. He was an alien.

After the shower incident, conversations were awkward, and it seemed that Legian and Sienna often only saw each other during the days. But every time he looked at her, he had the same look that he'd had in the shower. She found it both frightening and exhilarating.

Over the next month, she'd come back to their room and sometimes find a surprise he'd left for her. One time it was the Xbox and games from her cabin. Another time it was a painting of a forest to remind her of what was beyond the walls of the windowless base. She needed those moments since she was still the outcast; many Sephians eyed her like she was the alien.

It was near the end of her second month at the base when she made up her mind. She stripped out of her clothes and waited on the bed. When he opened the door, he stood and stared.

"Close the door," Sienna ordered, "and come to bed."

His look of shock morphed into one of pure excitement, and he then spent the day proving to Sienna that some pleasures were universal.

Legian never slept on the sofa again.

"You've been here for nearly a year already," Sienna said. "The Draeken have been here even longer, and who knows what they have planned. Time is running out to get my people on your side. It won't matter that you followed the Draeken here to stop them."

"It is still too early," Apolo said.

"If I was a Sephian—"

"But you are *not* a Sephian," he corrected.

Her lips thinned. "You're right; I'm not. I'm a human, and I know I'd want to meet aliens face-to-face rather than find out they've been skulking around for a year."

"We'll talk more tomorrow," Apolo said and turned from her.

She glared, stood, and left his room. Legian followed her to their room. Once inside, she plopped onto the sofa. "I'm sick and tired of no one listening to me because I'm human. They should be listening to me *because* I am human. I know my people, and they aren't fond of squatters."

"I agree with you," Legian said softly as he sat down next to her.

"That's great," she said dryly. "Now all we have to do is get Apolo to agree."

"I've been thinking about that." He paused for a deep breath. "I know of a way."

She spun to face him. "What is it?"

He reached out and clasped her hand in his. "If you were to accept to be my *tahren*, you would be recognized as a Sephian and become a member of the Sephian community."

She frowned. "*Tahren?* Like, soul mate? I thought that was a biological thing. I thought you can't choose your *tahren*. I thought the whole Sephian energy force thing chooses your *tahren* for you. You can't just pick someone to be yours."

He gave a small smile. "And you are correct."

"Legian, thank you for offering, but you can't do that for me. What if you find your *tahren?* No. I'll find another way."

He chuckled. "Sienna, I wish you could feel energy like I do. I knew you were my *tahren* the moment you touched me. I fought against the bond for so long, thinking it impossible for a Sephian and a human to become *tahren*, but I know now that it is real. I know not what lies ahead, but I do know that I'm not willing to sacrifice an opportunity given to me—to us —by the gods. You *are* my *tahren*. There is no mistaking that. I've only been holding off on informing Apolo until you had a chance to understand us better."

She sat there and said nothing as she considered his words. In his mind, clearly, his proposal included no subterfuge. She had feelings for him, but she wasn't sure if it was love or simply a blend of passion and friendship. Her brows knit together. Maybe there wasn't a difference.

After losing Bobby, she'd never wanted to care for someone enough to go through that kind of pain again. The problem was, she already did care for Legian too much.

She reached out and grabbed his hand. "So, you're my *tahren*. What do we do now?"

Chapter Four

S ienna walked into the country bar and scanned past the line dancers for the man she'd come to see, nearly missing him for the cowboy hat he wore. He had bellied up to the bar, drinking a frosty draft.

Tonight was her first mission. It had taken over a month for the Sephians to trust her enough to not track her every move and another two months before Apolo agreed to leverage her race. Unfortunately, as humans went, she brought few connections. Even though she'd done plenty of disaster response planning, most of her military involvement had been at the enlisted and noncommissioned officer level. Her best option was Bobby's unit.

Taking a deep breath, Sienna gave her late husband's friend a quick smile. Before walking over to him, she scanned the bar for anyone else from Jax's platoon. In her email, she'd pleaded for Jax to come alone, but he was a soldier first, which meant he wouldn't be alone.

Her gaze stopped on a man sitting in the booth at the other end of the bar. Sporting a buzz cut and sitting too uptight for a night out, the fifty-something man didn't fit.

She had no doubt the 51st Division, a joint Army-Air Force operations task force focused on space warfare, was here.

Straightening her posture, she considered walking right back out the way she came in. But Apolo was counting on her. Last week, a Draeken scout ship had been spotted flying over the base. If the Sephian base hadn't been discovered yet, it would be soon. It was just a matter of time.

She turned back to Jax and found his chair empty. Frowning, she spun around, only to come to a hard stop against a cowboy who filled out all ten gallons of that hat of his. A large hand latched onto her bicep, and she looked up into Jax's eyes. His hand lowered to her wrist. Their feet crunched on broken peanut shells littered across the hardwood floors as he led her through the bar and toward Buzzcut. Inside, frustration and fear prickled her.

"I told you to come alone," she ground out through clenched teeth.

"This is bigger than both of us."

"I know," she said. "But I'm trying to keep things from escalating too fast."

"I think it's too late for that," Jax said.

Buzzcut looked up from a barely touched beer when they stopped at his booth. The older man pivoted on his red bench seat, hopped to his feet, gave an overly generous smile, and held out a hand. "You must be Sienna Wolfe."

She inhaled before accepting the offered hand. "You must lead Jax's company."

"Among other companies. Major Sommers; at your service." He motioned to the booth and she slid in as he sat back down. Jax slid in next to her, effectively locking her in the booth.

Sommers put both elbows on the table and leaned forward over his beer. "Jax mentioned that you might like some assistance with some *illegal aliens*."

"I like to think of them as friends in from out of town," Sienna said. While anyone overhearing the conversation would assume they were talking about workers coming over from Mexico, they both understood the true meaning of his words. She glanced at Jax before turning back to Sommers. "How much do you know?"

He shrugged. "I know our *friends* have been here for some time, long before the night they took you."

She'd kept warning Apolo that the U.S. military wasn't half as dumb as he thought, but the Sephians had one major flaw: they thought they were smarter than everyone else. Not exactly an ego boost for a lone human in a bunker of five hundred-plus aliens. Then again, they'd won their freedom through blood, tears, and death. They earned a little self-righteousness, no matter how frustrating that could be at times.

"Why don't you fill me in on what you know?" Sommers asked.

Clasping her fingers, she leaned forward. She spoke as if her insides weren't tied in knots. "I was asked by Apolo—he's the Sephian leader here on Earth—to reach out to someone I knew and trusted in the military."

Sommers nodded. "You chose Lieutenant Jerrick because you knew him through your late husband."

She gave a quick glance to Jax. "Yes. Bobby trusted him, so I trust him."

"Your late husband was a trusted NCO in the 51st. I wish I'd had the chance to meet him," Sommers said before continuing. "Why don't you tell me more about Apolo and why he asked you to contact Jax."

There was so much to say, she struggled with where to begin. "Apolo wants to make official contact."

Sommers raised his brows. "Then why hasn't he contacted us?"

"It's not that easy. The Sephians don't exactly blend in, what with their gold skin and black eyes. Apolo knows that once they're out of the so-called closet, there's no going back. He wanted to take things slow and play their cards right."

"Invading our country is an act of war," Sommers cautioned.

Her jaw tightened. "They're not invading. They didn't even want to come here."

"They why are they here?" Sommers asked.

"They followed the Draeken here to prevent them from doing to us what they did to Sephia."

"And what did these Draeken do to Sephia?" Sommers asked.

"They enslaved the Sephians," she replied. "From what I've learned, the Draeken arrived on Sephia and conquered it during what they call the Great War. From what I got, this war was worse than all of ours thrown together, condensed into one massive attack. Anyway, the Draeken had advanced technology. They slashed the Sephian population in half within a couple weeks. For a couple centuries, the Draeken ruled with the Sephians as their slaves. Then, about twenty years ago, the Sephians rebelled in a drawn-out guerilla war that decimated both races. It was called the Noble War, and that was when they finally drove the Draeken from their world."

During all this Sommers listened but said nothing, so she continued.

"Kudos to the Sephians for getting their planet back. Bad news for us, because the next habitable planet along the space highway was Earth. Fortunately, the Sephians found out the Draeken had come here, so Apolo led a group of five hundred or so Sephians to a world they'd never heard of, a world they had no reason to care about, because they didn't want to see another world enslaved. And that pretty much sums up why the Sephians are here."

There was a long drawn out silence as Sommers seemed to ponder her words. "How many Draeken are here?"

"I don't know. Apolo seemed to think they escaped with only one ship and that it wasn't full. But it could still mean a few thousand."

He frowned. "If the Draeken came here to take over the world, then why haven't they tried to do so already?"

She shrugged. "Apolo thinks they're lying low to build infrastructure to implement their plans. He's been searching for their earthside base but hasn't found it yet."

"Hm." Sommers watched Sienna for some time. "You were held by the Sephians for over three months. How can you be sure you weren't fed a line of bullshit or that you weren't brainwashed? What if the Sephians are the ones after our world?"

"No." She shook her head. "They may have forced me to come to their base to keep their secret, but they've never harmed me, and everything I've seen aligns with their story. I don't agree with Apolo's decision to wait, but I understand why he did. Earth has no recorded visits from other worlds. Apolo was afraid we wouldn't be able to handle that knowledge. He's trying to do the right thing. When you meet with him, you can determine the truth for yourself. He's ready to meet. He *wants* to work with you to eliminate the Draeken threat."

Sommers leaned back. "I'm ready. Take me to his base tonight."

She stammered. "I can't."

"You can't or won't?" Sommers countered.

She swallowed. "Apolo does want to meet, but not at the base. He has concerns that the military would attack the base, and there are children there. He can't share the location of the base yet."

Sommers cocked his head. "This fellow wants to meet, but on his own terms. That's awfully convenient for him."

"I'm doing what I can. Give me your card, and I'll give it to Apolo."

"That's not good enough. I've got brass on my ass to get this situation under control. I need an assurance that Apolo will contact me *tonight*, and that his kind will show no hostilities."

"I'll stress the importance to him," she said, "but I'm just the messenger. Believe me, if I could get you in front of Apolo this very moment, I would."

Sommers eyed her for a moment before giving a tight nod.

She let out a sigh of relief. "Thank you."

Jax stood, allowing her to slide out and stand. As she turned to walk away, she noticed Sommers had said something as he lifted his beer. It wouldn't have been odd, except Jax was standing next to her, leaving no one near the major. *Ear piece*. She frowned. How many had just listened in on their conversation?

Jax followed her to the door. "I'll get you out of there, Sienna. I promised Bobby I'd look out for you, and I will."

She forced a small smile and patted his chest. "I'm where I need to be, Jax. The Sephians need me. I can save lives." She turned, threw open the door, and stepped into the cool night air. Grabbing the helmet off the seat, she hopped onto her Can-Am Spyder and peeled away from the curb, not quite confident whether she had just helped the Sephians or opened their back door to the proverbial wolf.

As she sped under flashes of streetlamps, it hit her that Jax and Sommers were the first humans she had spoken to in three months. It seemed like forever ago since she hadn't been the one the Sephians looked at like she was the alien. The normalcy of something as simple as a bar reminded her of the quiet, easy life she used to have.

She flogged the throttle to burn out the tension in her body. There was no going back. She didn't regret her choice to join the Sephians, not that she'd really had one to begin with.

A bike identical to hers pulled up alongside. Startled, she nearly drove off the road. She glared at the other rider. Legian's all-black garb and body shape was one she knew all too well. They drove side by side down the highway then down a winding country road, making turns every couple of miles until they reached a dead-end—their rendezvous point.

She climbed off her bike, pulled off her helmet, and scowled at Legian.

He'd removed his helmet and rubbed his head, the moonlight glistening off his skin.

"You were supposed to stay off the highway. What if someone saw you?" she said.

He motioned to his full suit. "And they would've assumed I was just another biker."

She shook her head. "You're lucky we weren't followed."

He reached into a chest pocket and pulled a small black device with two buttons, one blue and one red. He clicked the blue button. It lit up immediately.

Her jaw slackened. "Jax. I can't believe he bugged me."

"Your race is better trained than I anticipated," he said as he ran his hands over her.

"I guess they were serious about wanting to know the location of the base," she said, holding out her arms. "Damn it, I should've thought of that."

Legian stepped away and held up a tiny device. Legian dropped the tracker and shot it, sending dirt and leaves scattering. He watched the charred device smoke for a couple seconds before he holstered his blaster and clicked the red button. "This should block the signal from any other bugs."

She frowned. "You should've turned it on the moment I left the bar."

"I have no idea if it blocks human tech."

"Do you think they'll know we destroyed the tracker?"

"Yes." He turned to look down the dark road. "They're coming."

"I don't hear anything." She looked down the road, but couldn't see anything beyond the first curve. With the bike headlights off, the country night was black under a thick cloud cover. Exactly how Sephians liked it best.

"Three vehicles. About a mile off. Closing in fast."

"Call the base for an earlier pickup?" she asked.

"No time."

Chapter Five

"Into the woods," Legian said and took lead.

There was no mistaking the engine noise now. They were coming up fast and hard. Multiple big vehicles. Sienna followed Legian in the blackness, putting all her faith in his ability to find them a way out of this mess.

Legian helped her weave around trees. The engine noises cut, so he picked up the pace, and branches whipped at her from all directions. She could hear voices then the rustling of leaves as their pursuers began closing the distance between them. Adrenaline gave her added acuity, but she was still no match for the speed of the military guys on their tails.

"Stay safe."

"What?"

Without any additional warning, Sienna was sliding down a sharp decline. She landed hard and rolled back onto her feet. Legian had shoved her into a gully of some kind. She cautiously cocked her head from side to side. No whiplash. No broken bones. Still, her body was going to remind her of the fall in the morning. Legian tended to forget that she lacked the Sephian ability to heal.

"Legian?" she whispered.

No answer.

With the moon hidden behind clouds, she couldn't make out much in the darkness. She held out her arms and began to walk forward as fast as a nearly-blind woman could in a forest at night. She heard someone breathing fast above her, and froze. When the sound disappeared, she hurried forward, only to tumble over something and onto the ground.

Grabbing her now-throbbing shin, she leaned back against the fallen tree she'd catapulted over. To make matters worse, she found a soldier standing over her. His eyes were covered with night vision goggles, meaning he could see fine in the dark. He held a GPS-style device in one hand with a flashing bleep right in the center. The red light glinting off the nine-millimeter gun he held in the other. Damn. She had a second bug on her.

"Halo Two reporting. Target One attained. At least one unaccounted for. No tracking," the soldier spoke into the night air. It was Jax. "Halo One. Come in." He paused for a moment and looked around, his gun still trained on her. He tried to reach his unit several more times, and by the number of F-bombs he dropped, he wasn't getting the response he was looking for. "Are you okay?"

Sienna realized he was now talking to her. "Yeah, I think so."

"Good. Where's the one that was with you?"

"I'm alone."

"Then how'd you get two bikes out here?"

"He ditched me."

Jax continued to try to reach his unit.

She pulled herself up onto the log, yelped, and grabbed her leg. She winced and looked up at him. "I think my leg's broken."

Jax watched her for a moment then abruptly slid the gun into his holster and reached down to her.

As he went to examine her leg, she whipped out the Taser from the waistband of her jeans, shoved him off her, and zapped him. Electrical buzz filled the air as the two wires sent a violent charge into his chest. The shot lasted five seconds, but she imagined it felt like an eternity for Jax. When the burst stopped, he fell to the ground. She almost felt bad for him... almost.

Sienna pulled out a small cylinder that looked like a mini lipstick tube. Colorless, odorless, and potent. She bent over Jax and shook her head while he convulsed on the ground. "Sorry, but that's what you get for bugging me." She took off the cap and ran it across his neck the moment his hand grabbed her calf. Instantly, his grip relaxed, and his eyes fell shut. Jax would be out for hours.

Her leg throbbed. She may have exaggerated that her leg was broken, but it was close. She pulled the wires from his chest, retracted them into the Taser, and slid the weapon back into her waistband. She then felt around his neck for a transmitter, and realized it was an all-in-one earpiece. She tossed it into the darkness.

"Hey." A voice startled her from behind. She swung out, and he ducked. "Nice one." Legian sounded more pleased than pissed that she'd tried to punch him.

She pulled out her black bandana and wiped the sweat from her face, and then she looked up at Legian. "Where'd you go?"

"Leading the rest off-trail. I blocked their transmissions. Should buy us a minute or two before they regroup."

"So that's why Jax couldn't get a hold of them."

"This is Jax?"

She nodded. "But the blocker didn't work. He must've got a second bug on me because he used a GPS to find me."

She didn't want to ask, but she had to. "What do we do with him?"

"Leave him. We don't have time. I have a new rendezvous point."

"We can't leave him here. What if they don't find him? What if he gets bit by a rattlesnake or eaten by a bear?"

"The bears in this area are small. They could only gnaw on him."

"We'll take him to the base. Introduce him to Apolo."

"We could use a hostage."

"As a guest," she corrected. "Sommers didn't believe me. Maybe he'll believe one of his guys more."

After a brief moment of thinking through her words, Legian responded with his unique cross between a grumble and a sigh.

With a grunt, more for effect than strain, Legian lifted the unconscious soldier onto his shoulders, and they made their winding escape through the woods. The sounds of breaking twigs and crunching leaves were not far behind them.

Legian, carrying two hundred extra pounds, moved at a pace Sienna could keep up with. He remained in lead, using his natural night vision to guide them around trees and gullies. Sienna's leg throbbed with every step, but after several minutes, the pain lessened to a dull ache.

As they jogged, Legian called the base for an immediate pickup. She knew the soldiers would catch up them—they were trained for this sort of thing, and so it became a race to put enough distance between them to allow for a pickup.

Both Legian and Sienna panted as they continued through the woods.

Legian stopped and looked behind them. "They must be tracking us," he said in between breaths. "They're getting closer."

"It's me," Sienna said. "We should split up. I'm not a risk, but if they caught you..." Her words died in her mouth as she considered what the military could do to the first alien in their custody.

"Never," Legian said.

With perfect timing, a pale glow flashed three times just above them.

Sienna grinned. "They're here."

The silent shuttle touched down in a wider spot on a dry creek bed several dozen feet from them. The sound of slate cracking under its weight was welcoming. The door opened, and Legian and Sienna sprinted toward the ship. Legian, carrying Jax, entered first.

Shots rang out in the night, and Sienna ducked as she jumped on board. The door closed behind her, cutting off the sound of gunfire. She nearly collapsed with the feeling of safety in the dark ship.

"Made some friends tonight?" Nalea asked from the pilot's seat as she handed Sienna a pair of *drades*, the goggles that allowed night vision.

Sienna sighed as she slid on the glasses and the ship's interior came into full view. "I'll tell you about it later."

"I'm counting on it." Nalea lifted the ship from the ground.

Through the pilot's screen, Sienna could see at least a dozen troops entering the clearing, shooting at the bullet-proof hull as they did so.

Nalea pointed to the screen. "Look, they keep shooting at us like they can damage something."

"I need a second pair of *drades* for Jax," Sienna said.

"He doesn't need them," Legian grumbled from the back.

"*Guest,*" Sienna reminded him.

"Hold your hollies." Nalea rustled through a compartment. "I know I have an extra pair up here."

"It's horses," Sienna replied with a smirk to her friend.

Nalea spoke excellent English, but for some unknown reason, clichés and jargon threw her off every time.

Nalea rubbed her head. "Horses? Son of a bitch. I always mess that one up. Hold your damn horses, Sienna."

Sienna grinned and shook her head. And for some other unknown reason, Nalea picked up profanity and slang faster than a sailor could find a whore at port.

After a minute or so of opening and closing compartments, Nalea held out a second pair of glasses. "Strap in," Nalea said. "We'll be at the base in no time."

"Divert," Legian said from the back where he was disarming and securing Jax. "Sienna has a tracer somewhere on her."

"Sounds like you *really* made some friends," Nalea said. "Okay, I'm diverting now."

The ship twisted onto a new flight path, and Sienna held on to keep from falling.

Nalea pointed to a compartment near the ceiling. "There should be a scanner in there."

Sienna fumbled with the latch. Once open, she rummaged through the devices and pulled out one.

"No," Nalea said. "It's the black one."

"They're all black," Sienna said.

"No, most of them are various grays," Nalea countered.

Sienna held up another one.

"No."

A third one.

"Yes," Nalea said.

Sienna clicked the only button on the device and scanned her clothes. It flashed near her hip. She examined her waistband and found it on her belt.

She handed the tracker to Legian who dropped it into a trash compactor. Meanwhile, she scanned herself one more time to make sure Jax hadn't planted a *third* bug.

She went to put away the scanner, but Legian stopped her. He motioned to the unconscious soldier. "Scan him."

She stepped over to Jax and ran the scanner over him. The scanner vibrated over his forearm. She pulled up his shirt-sleeve and ran it over him again. Dammit, he was microchipped. "Uh, guys?"

"Use a blocker," Nalea said as she flew the ship.

"Blockers don't work," Sienna said.

"Use your knife," Legian said.

Her eyes widened. "You serious?"

"I'll do it," Legian said.

"No, I'll do it," Sienna said quickly. She didn't trust Legian to be gentle. She set down the scanner, pulled out her Swiss Army knife, and gulped. She ran her fingers across his skin several times. Only once she was sure she found the rice-sized microchip did she make a small slice and push it out. Immediately, she took her bandana and tied it over the bleeding wound.

Legian disposed of the microchip.

"All bugs are taken care of," Sienna called out.

"Returning to base flight path," Nalea said.

Sienna looked at Jax to see his eyes were now open. He was looking around, but she knew he couldn't see anything without night vision. "You're awake."

"You trying to slit my wrists?" Jax asked.

"You planted bugs on me. Call us even," she snapped back.

"You tased me," he said. "We're not even."

She slid the glasses onto his face for him since his hands were bound. Jax took in the high-tech cabin. She had to admit, the first few times she had been in a Sephian ship, she had also been in awe. Everything was so different from human planes. There were no keyboards of any kind. Every unused space was covered by smooth panels of dim screens.

Sienna wouldn't have known they were computer screens as opposed to just wall panels, let alone been able to read them, without the glasses. The ship was controlled by mental commands made through a band worn around the pilot's neck. Legian swore the technology was simple, but when he tried to explain it to her, it sounded anything but.

"Where am I?" Jax asked after a length.

"You're on a Sephian ship," Sienna answered. "You're going to meet Apolo."

He didn't answer, and he certainly didn't look pleased. If anything, he looked like the grim reaper had come for him.

Chapter Six

"You're not a prisoner," Sienna said.

"Then untie me," Jax said.

"No," Legian said.

Sienna moved to remove his restraints.

"Sienna, leave them," Legian said.

She looked up to see Legian, sitting directly across from Jax and pointing his blaster at him. She glared, knowing he would never shoot inside a ship. "Apolo wanted me to contact Jax. He's a guest, not a prisoner." She removed the rubber-like bindings.

She took a seat and watched Jax rub his wrists. She knew he must have had the same thoughts going through his mind that she'd had three months earlier when she stood outside a Sephian ship. Make a run for it or play along... for now.

He continued to look around the ship, clearly trying to ignore the blaster aimed at him.

Sienna broke the silence. "Pretty impressive, isn't it? The first time I was in one of these, I didn't have those night vision glasses so I was blind."

He pulled down the glasses then slid them back on.

"Draeken night shades," she said. "I call them *drades* for short."

"That's the worst slang word I've ever heard," Nalea said from the cockpit.

Sienna shrugged. "You're just jealous you didn't think of it."

"The Draeken came from a planet with a sun like ours, so they had to wear *drades* all the time on Sephia, where everyone lived on the dark side of the world. The Sephians are the opposite. If there's one thing I've learned about Sephians, it's that they like everything dark."

Sienna never could understand why the Sephians were so in love with dark colors. Maybe it was because they were a nocturnal race and had amazing night vision but could see less than a half-blind shrew during the day without corrective glasses. With oversensitive eyes, they kept everything insanely dim, even their computers. No wonder their skin sparkled.

"We're arriving at the base," Nalea said.

A minute later, the ship landed softly and silently on the base's hangar deck.

Sienna unbuckled her belts and helped Jax with his. When she headed to the door, Legian blocked her way. "Let me speak with Apolo first."

She frowned. "Okay."

He and Nalea stepped out to greet Apolo, while Sienna stayed back with Jax.

"What are the odds I get out of this alive?" Jax said softly near her ear.

"Good," she said quickly.

"You don't sound confident."

Problem was, she wasn't so sure.

Chapter Seven

Sienna and Jax waited just inside the ship as Apolo conversed with Legian and Nalea, two members of his trinity. His third member, Bente, stood to his right. Every Sephian leader had a trinity—a trio of their closest advisors. As usual, the Sephian leader wore the plain black Sephian uniform. No logos, decals, or emblems of any kind; there were no differences between uniforms. After being slaves for so long, it seemed as though the Sephians wanted little to do with hierarchy, though they did have a few ranks.

Apolo was the highest ranking Sephian male on both Earth and Sephia; his mate, the Sephian leader, was back on Sephia. No doubt the distance from his *tahren* accounted some for Apolo's dour mood. Tonight his dark hair, a touch longer than Legian's, was mussed, likely from running his hands through it. He oozed raw sex appeal. No wonder he had been snagged by the most powerful woman of the Sephian race.

After a couple minutes, Apolo placed a hand on Legian's shoulder as he passed him and walked toward the ship, stopping a few feet from its steps. Apolo motioned Sienna and Jax off the ship, and Sienna stepped forward, putting herself between Apolo and Jax.

Apolo tilted his head in her direction. "Thank you for taking such great risk for the Sephian people tonight. I'm glad to see you are unharmed, and I look forward to hearing what you've learned."

He then looked around Sienna to Jax and brought a hand to his heart. "Welcome to our base, Lieutenant." His words were, as usual, spoken in near-perfect English, with only the slightest Sephian stilt. "I apologize that your choice to come here was taken from you. My people can be often overzealous in protecting that which is important. You may call me Apolo. I know your people have two names. My people do not. We refuse to wear the slave names given to our ancestors by the Draeken. I am the *tahcaya* of the Sephian people. In your language, my position is somewhat comparable to a general."

Apolo then gestured to the large hangar. "As you can see, this base is our ship, which we've buried into the landscape for anonymity."

Jax remained stoic, silent. Sienna suspected the soldier still considered himself more a prisoner of war than a visitor. Much like she'd felt at first.

Apolo continued. "Despite the circumstances of your journey, I am pleased you are here. We have much to learn from one another. Rather than bombard you with questions, I believe you may be most comfortable first becoming acclimated to this environment. As your people say, make yourself at home. I will see to it that you have access to anything you need." He motioned to the third member of his trinity, who stepped forward. "Bente here will be your guide during your stay with us. First, he will see to it that you can communicate with your commander so that he is aware of the circumstances."

"What if I want to return to my unit?" Jax asked.

"I'll see that arrangements are made, should you wish to return. However, I hope you will stay for at least a few hours so that we can discuss how best for me to meet your commander."

Jax's eyes narrowed. "Three hours. No longer."

Apolo gave a small nod. His wrist-comm chimed, and he frowned. "I need to see to something. We will talk after you check in with your commander." Without waiting for a response from Jax, the Sephian leader turned and walked away.

"I'll show you where you can make a call," Bente said. He sounded polite enough, except Sienna knew Bente was anything but a nice guy. If Sienna were a gambler, she'd lay her money on the two being at each other's throats in five minutes flat.

"I'll go with you," she offered.

"Sure," Bente replied, and then motioned Jax down a hallway. "Pick up your feet, soldier. Try to keep up."

Where Nalea struggled with American vernacular, Bente had picked it up with ease. Sienna could almost see Jax's glare burning into the Sephian's back as he turned on his heel and followed his Sephian guide.

---

3 minutes later.

Bente shoved Jax against the wall. Jax twisted and slammed Bente against the wall.

Bente chuckled dryly. "You must have one hell of a death wish, human. You think you could take me on? Even if you got past me," he said with no sound of humor in his threat, "there's a base full of Sephians here who would skin you alive. You think you can take us all on?"

Jax wasn't backing down. Not one inch. "Try to knock me around again, and I guarantee you're going to be hurting."

Bente shoved him away. "If you put my people at risk, I don't give a flying fuck how you fight. I will put you down."

Sienna rolled her eyes. "Enough already." When neither moved, she glared at Bente. "Great job at making friends with humans, Bente. Way to go."

Bente narrowed his eyes before backing up a step. "Truce. For now." He held out his hand.

Jax looked at it for a very long moment then shook it. Bente patted Jax's shoulder, and it was like some pressure valve had been released. A bit, at least.

Bente started walking down the hall, and Sienna walked alongside Jax behind the Sephian. "I feel a man crush coming on. You two need some time alone?"

Bente belted out a laugh, and then muttered a curse in English.

"Geez, Ben. I know I didn't teach you that one. You've been watching too much cable," she said.

He shrugged. "Not much else to do around here."

"Do all you guys speak English?" Jax asked.

"And Spanish," Sienna answered. "Many can speak six or seven other languages already."

Jax frowned. "How long have you been here?"

"We studied your primary languages on our journey here. We also have weekly required language and humanities lessons," Bente replied, not directly answering Jax's question.

"The Sephian language is so complicated, picking up new languages is a piece of cake for them. Hell, I've been trying to learn Sephian for three months and still don't get it. And I've got two degrees and three languages under my belt."

"Or, maybe it's because we're smarter," Bente said before stopping at a closed door. He swiped his hand over a touchpad on the wall, and the door opened with a whoosh.

Inside, a young comm-tech sitting before several screens looked over his shoulder.

"Tanel," Bente began. "This is Jax. He needs to make a phone call."

"Oh. Okay," the comm-tech replied and motioned for Jax to come in. "I can place a call through the Internet using voice over IP. I just need a phone number."

Jax turned to Bente. "Or, you could just give me back my phone, and I could use that."

"You get your gear back when Apolo says and not before," Bente said. "So, do you want to make a call or not?"

Jax's eye ticked. "Yeah, I'll make the call." He headed into the room. When Bente followed, Jax added. "A little privacy?"

Bente smirked and stepped back out. "I can always listen to the call later."

"Bente," Sienna scolded. "You are not recording his call. How's that going to inspire trust?"

"It's okay, Sienna," Jax said. "I wouldn't have believed him if he said otherwise." He turned back to the comm-tech and made his call.

Bente and Sienna stood in the hallway. She could overhear the call, but Jax spoke in code—numbers and random words —indecipherable to her, but she imagined the comm-tech would spend the next few hours translating it. During the last bit of the call, Jax switched to normal dialogue. "They're treating me fine, and I'm going to talk with Apolo soon. I'll call you again when I can."

A moment later, Jax entered the hallway.

Sienna gave Jax a thoughtful look. "How's Major Sommers handling you being here?"

"I think he was surprised I was still alive."

"Probably because if positions were reversed, our guy would be dead already," Bente said.

"Nah," Jax said. "We'd run all kinds of tests first then kill you."

"We'd better get going. Apolo's room is on the other side of the base." Sienna rushed the words out before Bente could snap back a retort.

Bente smirked and motioned to Sienna. "After you."

She led them down the hallway. "This base is just the ship they came here in, so once you look at it like it's a spaceship, everything makes more sense. You can use the screens on the walls to pull up maps, find out where someone is, or call someone."

"But you don't have access," Bente added to Jax.

"You don't have access *yet*," Sienna clarified.

Jax's eyes narrowed. "You can see where anyone is at any time?"

Sienna nodded. "Yes. There are cameras everywhere except inside quarters, and the computers log every time you enter a room." She pointed to a touchpad. "See? Every room has one."

Jax looked at a touchpad on the wall like he was trying to process all the details of the place. "Everyone here military, or are there civilians based here as well?"

Bente answered. "All Sephians, regardless of age, are considered warriors. We do not have a formalized military function like you have."

"I noticed."

Sienna cocked her head. "What do you mean?"

"Haven't seen many guards. Most of the folks seem pretty casual. No one's geared up. This place doesn't look like a very secure base, especially for being an HQ."

Bente shrugged. "We're shorthanded. The Draeken controlled our world longer than our historical records date. All Sephians who have reached adulthood were born into slavery, so, for many of us, our military training was surviving the Noble War. We learn as we go." Bente pointed at Jax. "But make no mistake. Our lack of training is not a sign of weakness. Everyone around you is a survivor and will do anything it takes to stay that way. *Anything.*"

Jax ignored the veiled threat. "The Noble War. That where you fought the Draeken?"

"Yes, and we beat them. Our race was nearly destroyed, but the Draeken fared even worse. We estimate the few thousand who survived the Noble War jumped off-world in a mass exodus executed in a single night. We destroyed every short-range vessel that attempted to escape, but one of their core ships got away. We tracked it to Earth, which is how we ended up here to save you pale-skins."

Jax raised a brow. "We pale-skins have done a pretty good job at taking care of ourselves before you came along, Goldilocks."

"You haven't met the Draeken yet," Bente said.

"Maybe the Draeken aren't the bad guys," Jax mused.

Sienna butted in. "Trust me, they are."

Tamping down her frustration, she walked faster. Jax slowed as they passed a closed door that beautifully strange a cappella music emanated from.

Bente pointed at the door. "That room's off limits."

"It's where Sephians worship their gods. They are very protective of their beliefs," Sienna said. "The gardens are the next level down. They're gorgeous. Most of the Sephian food is grown down there. Hopefully, you stay long enough to see it."

"He isn't staying," Bente said.

She let out a breath. A little help from Bente would've been nice at improving race relations. Instead, he posed in his classic I-don't-give-a-shit stance. She ignored him and took the next right, which opened up into a massive space. She walked through the middle, ignoring the tables of

Sephians watching them. "Here's the Commons, where everyone eats. Pretty much just like any other cafeteria you've seen. Sephians are vegans, not that there's anything wrong with that, but they could learn a thing or two about spices. At least they have beer."

She opened the cooler and grabbed three beers, handing one to Jax and one to Bente. "Thought we could use some refreshments along the way."

Jax nearly smiled as he opened his can. "Smart girl."

Paying no attention to Jax or Sienna, Bente drank his beer as he watched a table of Sephian females who looked up from their chatter every now and then to flash him flirty smiles.

"Good to see your fan club made it, Ben," Sienna said.

He tossed the empty can into a receptacle. "Let's get you to Apolo's." He took lead through the Commons and the hallways beyond.

As they continued their walk, Jax looked around, taking in everything. Sienna wondered what his trained eyes noticed that she never had.

"This is a massive ship," Jax said.

"I still get lost." She motioned around them. "The rest of the base is mostly quarters or storage rooms.

"Do you have a brig here?" Jax asked.

Sienna thought for a moment then shrugged. "I don't think so. I've never seen any cells."

"We have a brig," Bente said. "But it's your lucky day. Since you're our *guest*, you get to bunk with me."

"Lucky me," Jax replied with sarcasm. "Do you have any Draeken in the brig?"

"Nope," Bente replied. "The only good Draeken is a dead Draeken."

Jax's gaze flashed to Bente before turning away.

"I've only seen one," Sienna said. "They'd have a harder time blending in than Sephians because of their wings."

Bente chimed in. "The Draeken have sickly pale skin, much like Jax here, but they tend to be taller. And, yes, they have wings."

Jax ignored the jab. "Wings would make any attempt to secretly infiltrate our world much more difficult. Can the wings be amputated?"

Bente nodded. "They can, and we've seen it done. But it's rare. Generally only half-breeds have it done. More out of shame than anything. It's rare a pure-blood would ever do it. Their wings are a source of pride, and proof of lineage is displayed across the skin. With how low their numbers now are, they would have to be desperate to go to such measures. Also, the wings are fully functional. To remove them is akin to removing a major organ. Their ability to take flight has given them a significant advantage in many battles."

"What are their key weaknesses? How did you defeat them?" Jax asked as if he were studying for an exam.

"We beat them with just enough luck and far too much sacrifice," a voice said from a doorway.

All heads jerked around to see Apolo step out into the hall. "Lieutenant, it's my hope that you can help bridge our peoples."

Jax gave a small nod. "I'll see what I can do."

Apolo gestured to his room. "I said we would talk, however, I gained some valuable information not long after you landed that we must address first. I'd like you to join me on this mission so you can see first-hand what we're up against." He looked across the three faces. "I have just learned the location of a Draeken camp."

Chapter Eight

Sephians. Draeken. Aliens. In no way could either pass as human, yet both were now inexplicably connected to Sienna's people. And here she sat, left behind in a makeshift underground base, as the two fought over her kind. One for domination, the other for freedom.

She felt so *useless*.

Sienna, as a noncombatant, was staying behind. Finding herself fidgeting nonstop, she headed over to the training room to burn off some energy.

As she hefted the blaster in her hand, she couldn't help but appreciate Sephian technology. She could shoot the hell out of a target without ever having to reload. And that was exactly what she did. She didn't know how long she fired, all she knew was that by the time she released pressure on the trigger, the target was nothing but smoking black ash. A burnt-metal scent and haze filled the room, but her patience hadn't improved.

At least she could hit the target. Shooting laser guns was completely different from shooting regular guns. Give her a twenty-two and she could nail a beer bottle from twenty yards. Laser guns, on the other hand, were much more sensitive and precise, even without the kick, making it nearly impossible to hit a target more than several feet away. Good for a sniper, bad for Sienna "Shotgun" Wolfe.

Even practicing a full hour every day, she still didn't have as good an aim with a blaster as she had with her Glock.

"Nice shooting."

She snapped around and grabbed at her heart with one hand. "Jesus, Lea. I could have shot you."

Nalea pursed her lips. "That would have been a mean thing to do. I don't think I would be your friend anymore if you did that."

"Yeah. Because you'd be dead."

"Your aim's not that good yet," she retorted.

"It's better than your clichés." She sighed and looked down at her watch. The ships should be arriving at the base any minute now. She walked over and set the blaster in its charger on the weapons wall. "I hope everything goes well."

"It will," Nalea said. "We hit the jackpop this time. Apolo's informant provided us with the location of their primary camp, and he's never fed us bad information before."

"First, it's jack*pot*, which further proves my point that my aim is far better than your clichés. Second, that's great news. If we could take a camp that big, we could handicap them in one blow."

"That's the plan."

Sienna thought for a second. "We could shoot some more while we wait, or... I have an unopened bottle of wine in my room."

Nalea grinned. "Wine, definitely."

"We'll grab it and head down to the gardens," Sienna said.

"That's the best idea I've heard all day."

They headed down the dim hallways toward her room.

About halfway there, alarms screeched and lights blinked in muted neon colors down the hallway.

"What's going on?" Sienna asked, glancing around.

The intercom answered her first. *The wards have been breached* was repeated over and over. Lucky for her, the Sephians had switched everything to English in a step toward integration.

Nalea and Sienna shot each other a quick look before the pair raced toward the tech-hub, and were the first to join the comm-tech on duty.

"Status," Nalea commanded.

The comm-tech started speaking in Sephian until he saw Sienna and switched to heavily-accented English. "Security has been disconnected at checkpoints *Ohni, Ufen,* and *Teni.* No reports from any checkpoints yet. Com-screens are also down everywhere. The entire base is off-grid."

"System failure?" Nalea asked.

"No. We verified. All systems are online," the comm-tech replied, stress crackling his voice.

"How could security just disappear in so many places at once?" Sienna asked.

"Invasion?" The words were no more than a whisper as they passed from Nalea's lips.

Sienna froze. Most of their troops were on the mission. The base was protected by nothing more than a skeleton force right now. They didn't stand a chance against any kind of large attack. "Have you notified Apolo?" she asked.

He gave her a blank stare. Sienna put her hand on the comm-tech's shoulders. "Tanel? That's your name, right?"

He nodded.

She looked him straight in the eye. "Tanel, have you contacted Apolo?"

Tanel wiped his brow with his forearm. "I tried, but all communications are blocked. I don't know what else to do."

"Keep trying. Let Lea or me know as soon as you get stats on what we're up against." She turned to Nalea. "We got to find out if it's Draeken or my people. Or Sephian. And how many."

Nalea nodded. "We need weapons."

"What is the protocol for emergencies?" Sienna asked Tanel.

"Um... Um..." Tanel stammered several times before reciting the emergency management plan. "All non-troops should lock themselves in their rooms—they should know that already. Then... Gods, I don't know. Apolo always handles everything."

The comm-tech looked like he was going to freak out. She grabbed his shoulders and looked him in the eye. "Okay, Tanel. It's going to be all right. Check the protocols. Use the base-wide communications to remind everyone of protocol. Lea and I will cover things until you can reach Apolo. Do you have some kind of portable unit that can't be cut?"

Tanel scrambled through a drawer and grabbed a couple of small devices. "These coms are used for system tests, so they're kept decoupled from the network. They're voice-equipped, so you can used them for communications."

"Good. If you need to reach us, use these." Sienna and Nalea helped each another fasten the devices to their clothing.

"Lock the door," Sienna commanded. "Let no one in but us. Got it?"

He nodded.

"You'll be safe here," Sienna called over her shoulder before stepping into the hall. The nervous Tanel was out of his chair and at the lock pad before Nalea was through the door.

Nalea pointed to a map on the wall. "The armory is near checkpoint *Ufen*."

They jogged down the empty hallway. They had yet to see another soldier. Shit had seriously hit the fan.

"*Ufen, Ufen.* That's D. Can't risk it; that one's off the grid." Sienna spoke her thoughts aloud. She came to a screeching halt and grabbed Nalea's arm, stopping her instantly. "The training room. It has plenty of weapons, and it's closer."

Nalea nodded. "Good idea."

And with that, they cut down the hallway to their left and were in the training room seconds later. They cautiously stepped into the large room and spread out. The facility was empty, and they ran to the weapons cabinet. Fortunately, all the lock pads still worked, and she followed Nalea's lead in grabbing weapons and gearing up even though Sienna hadn't trained with many of the weapons yet.

At that moment, Tanel's shaky voice came over the intercom, telling everyone to lock themselves in their rooms.

"Ready?" Nalea asked.

Sienna shoved a handful of hand restraints into the one cargo pocket that wasn't chock full of weapons. She did one final check before looking up. "Ready."

Nalea poked her head into the hallway. "Clear."

Sienna stepped forward, and her back pocket zapped her with a tiny electrical bolt. She fumbled for the comm that could double as a portable bug killer. Nalea had hers out and to her ear already.

"Go," Sienna commanded into the flimsy bookmark-shaped device.

"It's the Draeken," the comm-tech said in a rush. "They're everywhere. It's impossible. How'd they—?"

"Calm down, Tanel," Sienna spoke into her com. "How many are there?"

"Don't know. Dozens. More."

Not good. "Where are they now?"

"Looks like they are all moving toward the Commons from the three checkpoints."

Nalea frowned. "But there's nothing at the Commons. Why are they moving away from the armory?"

"They have to go through there to get to the tech-hub and the officer quarters. Or, ah, shit. Of course."

"What?" Nalea asked.

"They plan to set up shop in the Commons to divide and conquer the base." With the exception of a few smaller hallways that connected the larger hallways like strands of a spider's web, the ship was set up according to a hub-and-spoke pattern, with everything coming together at the Commons. The Draeken would effectively cut off all areas of the base from each other then sit and wait for Apolo to return. They could decimate the Sephian force in one blow with minimal casualties on their side.

"Good work, Tanel. Keep us posted." Sienna slid the comm back into her pocket.

"We can't let them take the Commons. If Tanel can't get a hold of Apolo to warn him..." Nalea didn't finish. Sienna couldn't blame her; they both knew the outcome already, and it didn't need to be put into words.

The lights all brightened. Nalea winced, and Sienna pocketed her *drades*. "They've accessed the light systems," Nalea said, shielding her eyes with one hand.

With the Sephians blinded, the Draeken could practically waltz in and take the base with no casualties on their end. For this situation to happen when half the Sephians were off base, there was no way it was coincidental. Decision time. She grabbed Nalea's arm. "Okay. You find some sunglasses and head to the checkpoints that didn't show breaches to pull together what's left of our forces into something that can take on the Draeken. Since I can see, I'll try to beat the Draeken to the Commons and block them."

"You can't possibly think to hold off the Draeken on your own."

"Maybe, maybe not; but I can at least buy you time to bring in the cavalry."

Nalea watched her for a moment then nodded. "Kill on sight."

"Damn straight." As they split to go down separate hallways, Sienna paused and turned to face her friend. "Hey, Lea?"

"Yeah?"

"You better not drink that wine without me."

"Wouldn't dream of it." She gave Sienna a smile that was all too quickly erased by battle-hardened features before disappearing around the bend of the hall.

Sienna was alone; completely, utterly alone against an alien force she didn't stand a chance against. She'd only seen one Draeken before—the scout Legian had killed who, without Legian's action, would've killed Sienna. She reached for the com. "Update," she commanded.

"Looks like each group is a full squad. Twelve in each. There are at least four groups, maybe more. The *Ohni* group will be there soon, within a few minutes at most. Some med-techs blocked the hallway. It slowed them down a bit. The other two groups are farther back. Looks like some of our folks are fighting back."

Without another word, Sienna sprinted toward the Commons. There was no sound as she approached the large, open area, not even the usual noise of pots and pans clanging in the kitchen.

Looking around the room filled with enough tables and chairs to seat half the base, she turned back to the kitchen. It was the only place where she wouldn't be a sitting duck. With a hop, Sienna hoisted herself over the waist-high counter and gauged her surroundings. The ceiling was ten feet high. It would limit the intruders' ability to fly, and she could use all the help she could get.

She set two blasters on the counter in front of her. One human against thirty or more winged aliens—she'd have better odds of winning the lottery. She shook her head. All she needed to do was delay the Draeken until Nalea brought in the reinforcements.

A noise came from hallway *Ufen*. The temperature in the Commons seemed to skyrocket, though she knew it was from her adrenaline. More sounds followed: boots thudding, weapons clanging, clothes rustling. It grated against her nerves. *Show time.*

She wiped sweaty hands on her pants before reaching into a pocket and pulling out a small disc. A Draeken chaos-charge. She examined it with irony. A taste of their own medicine would serve the bastards right.

When the first Draeken came into sight, she nearly dropped the charge. Sienna had forgotten how intimidating they were. Taller than even the Sephians, with silver hair, gray eyes, and skin covered by complicated weaves of colored designs; not to mention those wings. There was nothing else like it. The wings were huge, taller than each soldier. Even tucked in, they were the same width as each Draeken. It was terrifying and beautiful in a fallen angel kind of way.

As they started to spread out, she swiped her finger down the ignition pad and threw the disc into the center of the squad. The charge was designed for use against Sephians, but she was counting on the fact that the thing wouldn't be pleasant for its creators, too. The moment the charge hit the ground, she crouched behind the counter, closed her eyes, and held her hands to her ears. Even so, the sound was deafening when the charge exploded in an eruption of light brighter than the sun and a sound like a harpy's screech.

When she could bear it, she pulled her hands from her

ears and picked up the blasters. She jumped up and began shooting like she'd gone insane. The Draeken, with blood oozing from their ears, staggered from the blast, knocking down tables and crawling behind them. Two Draeken went down beneath her first spray of shots. The remaining Draeken fired back, and she ducked behind the counter. Their shots cut through the wall like fire through papier-mâché. Her heart lurched in her chest. What the hell kind of technology did these guys have?

Scrambling to the next counter, Sienna pulled out a second charge. Only this one wasn't a Draeken charge. This one had been created by the Sephians, and she hated it; it reminded her of the dark ages, when lives had mattered so very little.

Voices, sounding muffled, were approaching.

Don't hesitate. She raised herself enough to send another barrage of shots across the open area. At least one shot made it home, because she heard a grunt followed by yelling. She shimmied across the floor back to the original counter. *Can't let them get a bead on me.*

Sienna simultaneously pushed two buttons on the blood-charge before throwing it over the counter. Like the chaos-charge, accuracy didn't matter on this one. She curled into a fetal position. Shouts and sounds of scrambling Draeken filled the air. Clenching her fists, she prayed she was safe behind the counter.

There was no sound when the blood-charge exploded. The screams were the only way she knew it had gone off. And there were plenty of those. She waited for several seconds after everything became deathly silent before she warily pulled herself to her knees and peered over the counter. The entire squad had been killed. Hundreds of tiny x-shaped spurs stuck out of their bodies and wings.

The marks left on their skin were identical to the scars

Legian had gained during the war. His squad had been discovered while sabotaging a Draeken base. The only two survivors, Bente had dragged Legian into the woods, where they had played hide-and-seek with the Draeken for days until they were rescued. Legian had been lucky. If it hadn't been for Bente to pull energy from, he never would have lived.

A couple of the Draeken still moaned. She felt pity for them. The spurs were coated with a deadly cocktail of anticoagulant and poison designed specifically for Draeken physiology. They were already dead; their bodies just didn't know it yet.

Her pity didn't last long. A shot whizzed by her ear, signaling a second squad already spreading out into the room.

Dammit. Where is Nalea?

She felt in her pockets for another charge. No more.

"*Nuleet*," a Draeken called out. He said something else, but she couldn't make out the strange curt words that reminded her of the German language. Everything fell silent.

Building courage, she peeked around the corner of the counter, and found herself looking right into the eyes of a large Draeken with long, mussed silver hair.

He arched his brow. "Human?" He spoke in clear, nearly perfect English, with barely a hint of that German-like accent. The Draeken sounded genuinely surprised at seeing her. "Surrender. You are sorely outnumbered."

"Don't be so sure. That last squad didn't last long," Sienna called out from behind the counter.

"There's no honor in using a blood-charge. Only Sephian scum would resort to that." The Draeken had the nerve to sound pissed off.

"Then how about you surrender?" she replied.

The Draeken guffawed. "To whom? I don't see Apolo here."

She gritted her teeth.

"If you surrender now, we will not hurt you. We have no intentions of harming humans. We came here in peace."

"Yeah, sure you did," Sienna replied dryly. Except her insides were twisted like a wet towel wrung too tight. She wasn't going to delude herself; she knew there was no getting out of the mess she was in.

His wings ruffled in obvious irritation. "Have it your way then."

He made a motion with his hands, and his squad spread out. At that moment, the third squad appeared, looking a little worse for wear. One against twenty-four. Even after obliterating the entire first squad, her odds hadn't improved much.

A hurricane of shots flew through the kitchen, and she scurried to hide between the ovens and refrigerators. Before she reached a safe place, heat blasted her, and a sharp pain cut through her left thigh. She cried out and dropped to the ground. Blood poured from the wound, even though the blast had cauterized the skin around it. So much blood. *No! Don't let it be an artery.*

She was surprised the wound didn't hurt more, though she suspected she was in shock. She pulled out a hand restraint and tightened it around her thigh. The makeshift tourniquet would buy her a few extra minutes at most before she passed out from blood loss.

Her attackers must have heard her scream because the shooting stopped. She clenched a gun in her hand. The silence scared her more than the gunfire.

"Keep moving," Sienna repeated like a mantra. With a heave, she dragged herself back to the front. Out of nowhere, a boot came down on her injured leg, and she screamed in blinding agony.

When her vision cleared, she found herself lying on her back, the Draeken who had spoken before now towering over her. He got down on one knee, watching her with silver eyes, then grabbed her gun and yanked her to him.

"So, have the humans allied with the Sephians?"

Her strength siphoning from her body, she didn't respond. He continued to watch her. A laser cut through a wing and he swung back against the sink, the plastic shattering.

"Sienna!"

She pulled herself up to see Nalea running toward her. Sienna had never seen a more beautiful sight in her life. The sounds of battle echoed from the cafeteria.

"It's about time." She reached out for the gun the Draeken had taken from her, which he'd dropped when Nalea shot him.

Nalea gave her a full smile before giving the fallen Draeken a solid kick to the gut. He let out a grunt. She grabbed a fist of his hair and yanked. "Roden." She spat the name with vile surprise.

Even though his brow was furrowed in pain, he smiled. "I see my reputation precedes me."

"You will pay for what you've done to my people." She pulled out her gun and aimed. His leg kicked out, knocking her down.

"Lea!" Sienna's scream came out more like a whisper. Somehow, she pulled herself up on an elbow to helplessly watch as the two clashed, too weak to help. They were too close for her to shoot. All she could do was wait for a clear shot as her friend fought an opponent who clearly outmatched her in both size and skill.

Time seemed to slow as the two fought. Roden knocked

Nalea to the ground, his wings blocking Sienna's view. They paused for a lengthy second as though frozen then Nalea twisted and came up with a blade, slicing across his shirt. His punch connected, and Nalea fell back.

With the last of her strength, Sienna fired a shot above his head, and pieces of ceiling rained down onto his wings, hitting his wound. He hissed and strode toward her.

"No." Sienna fired again. Missed. He kicked the gun out of her hand, and his boot shoved her hard. She felt herself hit the wall, and her breath burst from her lungs.

As she lost sensation in her limbs, Nalea filled her vision.

"Glad you could make it," Sienna whispered hoarsely, no longer having enough strength to talk.

"Stay with me, Sienna. Stay with me."

"We make a good team, don't we?"

"Yeah, Sienna. We do."

Those were the last words she heard before the world closed in on her.

Chapter Nine

I'm in hell.

That was Sienna's first thought when she regained consciousness. Her head throbbed. Her mouth tasted like cotton. Every muscle in her body ached. She opened her dry eyes, but the room was dark.

When she moved to pull her body upright, hot pain shot through her leg.

"Ow," she muttered hoarsely.

"Careful, *tahren*." Legian's arms enveloped her and pulled her gently into a seating position. "Here." She felt Legian wrap her hand around a glass. He coaxed it to her lips, and she nearly coughed when the cool liquid splashed her throat.

"That's enough for now." He pulled the glass away too soon and wiped water from her chin with his finger.

Sienna lay her head back against the pillow.

She was alive, which meant that, by no small miracle, they'd held back the Draeken. And Legian was here. He'd survived. She reached out, and he grabbed her hand.

"It's too dark," she said.

She heard a click, and suddenly she could see him in the

light from a small beaded lamp at her side. He squinted in the light but continued to look at her.

He was frowning. "I wish you had the Sephian ability to pull energy from others to heal yourself."

"I wish so too." She instinctively looked around for a window, even though she knew there were none. Where everything else on the base was shades of gray and black, in the medical ward, silky fabric draped the walls and all the furniture was soft. Even the plush mattress she lay on was nothing like a hospital bed. Everything was more like a surreal lounge instead of the chemical-laden cleanliness of hospitals she'd known.

Jax yawned in the corner and came to his feet. "You're awake."

Sienna turned, but her neck muscles were too stiff, and she closed her eyes. "How long have I been out?"

"You've been in the med-hub for four days," Jax said.

Four days?

Legian spoke. "The first two days were hard. Fayel didn't think you would pull through. But I told him you would. You don't know how to give up."

"I told him the same thing," Jax said.

She gave a weak smile. "I'm glad you stuck around, Jax, instead of heading back to your unit."

He shrugged. "Sommers wants to keep a man on the ground here. I was reassigned to advise Apolo."

More likely, he was reassigned to keep tabs on Apolo, Sienna thought to herself. "So, what did I miss? Did everyone make it?"

"Nalea brought you here after the attack," Legian said. "She saved your life. We suffered minimal casualties on the base; all thanks to you, from what I've heard. But, gods, Sienna. When I learned you faced the Draeken… on your own, no less…"

As his words trailed off, Sienna closed her eyes when she remembered. "All I did was cause a distraction until Nalea could get there with reinforcements."

"Distraction?" Jax guffawed. "You took out an entire Draeken squad on your own."

Legian smiled. "It seems that my *tahren* is the now the most beloved human on this planet."

"Hi, Jax," a woman said sweetly.

Jax gave her a friendly wave. "Hey."

Sienna looked up to see a petite, Sephian female enter the room. Like all med-techs, she wore colorful clothes. On Sephia, everything was tied to energy. Med-techs were more about donating energy to those who needed it than actual patch-ups. It was a glossy example of how, in some ways, Sephians and humans really were from two different worlds.

"Don't mind me," she said when she approached the foot of Sienna's bed. "I'm Risa. I'm just here to check your bandage."

"Do you mind, Legian?" Risa asked, shielding her eyes from her lamp.

Legian clicked off the lamp.

Now enveloped in darkness like that of a night with a full moon, Sienna felt the med-tech fidget with the bandage that covered most of her left thigh. Her teeth clenched, and she sucked in a breath.

"You're lucky to still have your leg, let alone your life," Risa said. "If Jax hadn't been here to transfuse blood, you might not be here. We were very lucky his blood worked. It's too bad you don't have our ability to heal. It would save you a lot of time and pain."

"So I've heard," Sienna gritted out, and threw out, "Thanks, Jax. Now, we're even."

"Not even close," he said.

Risa continued. "You're human. Do what humans do.

Embrace the pain. It means you're on the road to recovery. Though, you'll be lucky to walk again."

Sienna frowned. "I don't believe you."

"Who's wearing the medical uniform?" she replied curtly.

Sienna swallowed. "Doc thinks I will be able to walk again, right?"

"You'll walk again," Jax said with confidence.

Legian spoke. "Sienna, there was considerable muscle damage. Fayel believes that, with physical therapy, you may be able to walk again with the help of a full leg brace."

"I'll walk again," she said to reassure herself before changing the subject. "How'd the mission go?" When no one responded, she asked, "What happened?"

"Your leg is looking better. I'll be back to check on you a little later." Risa grabbed her gear and left the room in a rush. On her way out, she added. "Maybe I'll see you at dinner, Jax?"

"Yeah, sure. See you then," Jax said.

Sienna turned back to Legian. She'd prayed their mission was a dull hop around the patch. Her gut told her that her prayers hadn't been answered. "Legian, turn on the light so I can see you."

The lamp clicked on, but he had his face turned away from her.

Jax watched Legian with a hooded gaze, clearly waiting for the other man to speak.

She turned to Legian. "Tell me what happened."

When she thought he wasn't going to answer her, Legian finally spoke. "It was a trap. And, like blind children, we walked right into it. The intel showed the Draeken camp to be in a deep valley. We thought it was perfect for an attack. We didn't realize until it was too late that there was only one way in and out of the valley. It was a bottleneck. A perfect ambush. They came at us from above and below. We didn't stand a chance. Over half our ships were destroyed in the first minutes. Only four ships escaped safely."

Four? There had been five times that many. "Oh, Legian, I'm so sorry," she whispered. She wanted to hold him, but he had distanced himself.

He continued. "We lost nearly two hundred troops and any military advantage we may have had. Jax and I escaped only because we were with Apolo. Another ship allowed themselves to be slaughtered so we could escape. Fifty Sephians sacrificed their lives to save ours." His hands covered his face. "We ran, while our people were slaughtered."

"Don't," she whispered, frowning. "Don't tarnish their sacrifice. It was their choice. They gave you a chance to survive to defeat the Draeken next time."

He paused at her words then continued. "In one brilliant strike, the Draeken crippled us. We were overconfident after pushing them off Sephia. We don't stand a chance against them now." He stopped, turned to her, and then turned the other way. Like he was trying to escape the demons in his mind.

"It will be okay," she said, not knowing what else to say. Without Apolo, the Sephians would be lost, but she knew that as long as Apolo lived, the Sephians wouldn't break apart.

He swung back to her. "No, Sienna. Don't you understand? We have failed. I have failed you, your world, and your people. I should have seen the trap. Instead, I let myself become proud. Too proud to think the Draeken may be one step ahead. Too proud to consider we might not stop them. We've never been able to stop them, only run them off... and now it's too late for your world."

"You're wrong; you haven't failed. We'll stop them. My people outnumber them by billions. Our military is strong—"

"Do you really think your people stand a chance against the Draeken if they want this world?"

"Yes, I do," she said with conviction.

"I do, too," Jax echoed. "We're stronger than the Sephians give us credit for."

Legian shook his head. "You don't know the Draeken. Not like I do. They're not like any opponent your world has ever faced. Their technology is too advanced. Everything we have, we've taken from them." He paused. "I had a sister. Did I ever tell you that?"

Sienna blinked. "No, you didn't. What's her name?"

"Her name was Cepa. She was beautiful. Some even compared her to Krysea. Cepa was five years younger than me and had more spirit than a pack of wild *fregee*. Ah, the messes she got us in." He chuckled, shaking his head, and then sobered. "A Draeken wanted her for himself. It was the master's son. It didn't matter that she'd already found her *tahren*."

Sienna sucked in a breath. In the corner, Jax's features were tight as he listened.

Legian continued, as if he were talking to himself. "When the master's son came to take her, Cepa's *tahren* managed to kill him. But he was killed as well. Cepa was devastated. She tried to end her life, but the master claimed her for himself as punishment and proclaimed that she was not to be allowed to die. During the final battle, when I found her, what I found was a shell that looked like my sister. Cepa's spirit had fled with her *tahren*'s. I did the only thing left a brother could do. I helped her body join her spirit."

"Oh, Legian. I'm so sorry," Sienna said.

His head lifted as though it weighed a hundred pounds. "That's what the Draeken do. They claim everything, and they won't grant you peace of death until they've taken everything worth taking. How can you beat that?" Legian looked pointedly at Sienna and Jax in turn.

Sienna swallowed. "Your people beat them once. Now it's my people's turn. We'll succeed. With Sephian knowledge and guidance, we can beat them. Together, we *will* beat them."

He crossed his arms over his chest as though to challenge her. "And you believe that?"

She nodded. "Absolutely."

Chapter Ten

Two weeks later.

Sienna leaned on her cane for support. She was at Legian's side, finding it impossible to stand still. Her adrenaline was too amped up. She found herself fidgeting, so she tucked her free hand in her pocket. She'd never been to any event as important as this one.

Getting to stand at Apolo's side, she was being afforded an incredible honor, even though it was for show. Similarly, Jax stood at Apolo's other side. She glanced over at Apolo and Jax. Straight as soldiers, neither looked the least bit stressed.

They reminded her so much of Bobby right then. He'd been a gunnery sergeant under Jax. Bobby and she hadn't been married long enough for her to get to know many in his unit. She'd been ready to follow Bobby wherever he was stationed, but a teenaged driver, driving while texting, had changed everything in an instant.

The doctors had said Bobby never felt a thing. One second he was walking across a cross-walk, the next, he was taken from her forever. Just an ordinary accident. Sienna had quit her job the following week; two months later she sold their loft, and began construction on her cabin. She'd had enough of a world that no longer made sense; had enough of the bullshit. She wanted to be alone. Alone was safe. Alone didn't break her heart.

Then something happened that went against all the plans she'd made and all the promises she'd pledged to herself. Just when she thought she had reclaimed control, Legian had literally crashed into her life and thrown all those plans to hell. She knew now though that helping the Sephians gave her renewed purpose. She was exactly where she needed to be.

The huge hangar doors began to open, jarring her from her reflections. The loud *whoomp-whoomp* of a large helicopter reverberated around the space. She watched in awe as the Chinook settled through the doors and onto the open ramp below. It dwarfed the Sephian ships, and she wondered if Apolo was ready for the change touching down on the landing pad.

It seemed to take forever for the huge blades to stop moving. Sienna's heart thumped in her chest as she willed herself to calm down. She'd told Apolo so many times that he could trust humans. Apolo was stuck behind the proverbial eight ball; his troops had been decimated, he'd lost touch with his spy, and they didn't stand a chance against the Draeken alone. Now, humanity's future teetered on humans accepting the Sephians. Jax had updated his CO every day, but still, today would be a moment of reckoning.

At least two dozen troops, all dressed in black fatigues with matching emblems on their shoulders, poured out of the helicopter. The colonel had come prepared. Even though the Sephians still outnumbered them twenty to one, Sienna had no doubt the officer had more than enough reinforcements waiting an arm's reach away to take the base if necessary. She prayed it wouldn't become necessary.

One of the last of the group to emerge, the colonel stepped out of the helicopter, safely encircled by his soldiers. It was easy to recognize him; even in basic black, there was a presence about him, that indefinable air of confidence that surrounded all strong leaders.

Sienna immediately recognized Major Sommers behind the officer, and realized this was Jax's platoon, plus more.

The pair walked toward Apolo's group, a wall of men flanking them on both sides. The colonel stepped with intent as though he was attending a ribbon cutting ceremony rather than stepping on alien territory for the first time.

Jax stepped forward, meeting them halfway, and saluted. "Welcome to the Sephian base, Colonel Jerrick, sir."

Jerrick? She furrowed her brow while she examined the officer. Gray buzz cut where Jax's was brown. Both had the same chocolate eyes. Same nose, same chin. The older man even had the same saunter. That was why he had seemed so familiar. He had twenty or so years on his son, but the resemblance was uncanny.

The colonel was speaking. "Good to see you, Lieutenant. How have they been treating you?"

"I have been treated fairly and with respect, sir."

The officer watched him for a moment, as if he were gauging the sincerity of Jax's words. Then he nodded. "Good to hear. Now, let's get this show started." He turned his attention on Apolo and approached the Sephian leader.

Jax motioned to Apolo. "Colonel Jerrick, this is Apolo, leader of the Sephian force here on Earth." Jax said the last word with a slight hesitation, like he'd never used it in an introduction before, which he probably hadn't. "Apolo, this is Colonel Jeremiah Jerrick, commanding officer of the 51st Joint

Special Operations Task Force, a battalion operating within the U.S. Space and Strategic Defense Command."

Apolo held an open hand out to the officer. "It is a pleasure to meet you, Colonel. Having your son as our guest these past couple weeks has been a tremendous opportunity for us to learn from one another."

The officer returned a hearty handshake. "I look forward to our conversations. And I'll warn you—I won't beat around the bush. That's not my style. I have plenty of questions. And I'm expecting even more answers."

Apolo nodded. "I would expect as much. I have placed the safety of this base and its three hundred souls in your trust."

"A gesture well received," the officer replied.

"Now, if you'd like to come with me, I have a room for us to talk candidly. We have much to discuss." Apolo gestured down a hallway.

The officer nodded. Bente and one of the officer's men stepped in front, and the two leaders walked away side by side, with their officers falling in behind and the remaining soldiers forming up around them.

A dark-skinned soldier sidled up next to Jax. He gave Jax a salute then a smile that was quickly returned.

"Staff Sergeant, it's good to see you," Jax said.

"Lieutenant," he replied.

The pair stepped in line behind the officer and Apolo, and Legian and Sienna followed after.

Sienna was far enough behind the leaders that she couldn't make out their words. Not that she tried. She assumed it was casual chit-chat, as they would wait to reach Apolo's secure quarters to get into negotiations. She hobbled with her cane to keep up with the group.

"Yltar!" a young Sephian yelled as he jumped out into the hallway. Everyone froze. Standing before Apolo and the officer was a young Sephian man holding a blood-charge.

Bente and a soldier stood on either side of the man, both poised to attack. The sounds of bootsteps and movement erupted around Sienna.

"Giphers. Give me the charge," Apolo commanded as he stepped between the officer and the newcomer.

The Sephian shook his head, and he started to cry. "I'm sorry. I have no choice. They've got her. They've got Giras."

"Who has your sister, Giphers?" Apolo asked gently, yet his voice clearly demanding an answer.

"They'll kill her if I fail. My life for hers, they said." Tears streamed down his face, and he scowled. "We shouldn't have come here. They need us on Sephia. Let the humans deal with the Draeken. We don't owe them anything." And with that, Giphers moved his fingers, and the blood-charge lit up. He tossed the device in the air. He lowered his head to his hands and wept.

Legian threw Sienna to the ground. He landed on her leg, and sharp pain tore through it. She gasped as she tried frantically to move.

Everything seemed to move in slow motion as the charge armed over a two-second timer. Apolo dove for the hovering charge while Jax and the staff sergeant tackled the officer. Apolo grabbed the charge and threw it away down the hall as Bente covered him. It exploded in mid-flight, exactly as it was designed to do.

Sienna had never seen a blood-charge go off before. Not even when the Draeken had attacked the base. It was bizarre seeing an explosion without any sound. At first, it looked like dust filled the air. But she knew that small x-shaped barbs were in that poisoned dust, and they flew everywhere.

Giphers collapsed. Apolo and Bente hit the floor hard. Several others still on their feet fell to the ground, grasping at wounds she could not yet see.

Then the world returned to normal. Blood splattered the walls. Men yelled and moaned.

"Sienna? Sienna, are you hurt?"

She looked up into Legian's concerned eyes at the same time she felt his hand against her cheek. "I'm fine." Her dazed words came out like a shout. "You okay?"

His look of relief was instant and brief. The next instant, his frown returned and he jumped up and ran toward Apolo.

Sienna saw Sommers on the floor, and she scrambled to him. He held a bloody hand to his shoulder. She reached out to him. "Are you okay, Major?"

He winced. "Been through worse. What the hell was that?"

Rather than answer, she yanked off the bandana tied around her wrist and pressed it against his shoulder. "We need to get you to the med-hub."

"Don't move!" The muzzle of a gun pressed into her temple.

Sienna froze.

Chapter Eleven

"You better not move," the major said. He placed his hand over hers and pulled away with a wince, keeping pressure on his wound while removing her hand from under his. Her bloodied hand fell to her pants, and the cold metal barrel nudged harder against her temple.

She looked out of the corner of her eye since she couldn't turn her head. Golden and crimson blood splattered the walls, mixing together to form bizarre abstract art. Men lay on the floor and leaned against walls, gritting their teeth against the pain of their injuries. Sephians aimed blasters at the soldiers, who in turn aimed guns at the Sephians. The whole situation had become a face-off.

Sienna spotted Legian out of the corner of her eye, and he looked furious while he knelt by a wobbly Apolo and pressed his hand over his leader's arm. Blood continued to ooze out, which meant it had been a very serious injury. Bente was down, and at least a dozen rifles were pointing at them.

With Legian's help, Apolo pulled himself to his feet. She was impressed that the man was even conscious after losing so much blood. He seemed unfazed by the guns pointing at him. He turned to face the colonel, who fortunately looked like he had pulled through the incident unscathed though it was difficult to tell.

With the worst timing, the entire staff of med-techs came racing around the corner. Many weapons swung in their direction, but through either a miracle or training, no shots were fired. The med-techs stumbled to a stop, dropping supplies and nearly tripping over each other. They stared wide-eyed, looking from Apolo to the fiasco and back again. Risa was near the back of the group, flat against the wall.

Apolo held his uninjured arm toward the med-techs. "Allow my people to help your injured men. Their blood will not clot without the antitoxin. Anyone injured will die without assistance."

The colonel looked over his bloodied men then nodded tightly.

Apolo motioned to the dozen or so med-techs. "It was a blood-charge. Help the humans first. And get Bente to the med-hub fast." Two raced toward Bente, who lay unconscious on the ground, blood pouring from his back. They had him on a stretcher before the others gingerly stepped forward and spread out among the injured.

A young med-tech rushed to Apolo and swabbed him—the Sephian version of injections—with the antitoxin. Apolo stopped her when she rolled up her sleeve. "Help the humans first. Put the call out for more donors to heal the wounded Sephians."

"But... you're hurt," the med-tech stammered. "You are our highest priority."

Apolo glared at her. She paled, turned, and hustled to a fallen American soldier. Legian grabbed a cloth binding out of her bag and wrapped it around Apolo's arm to staunch the blood. Then, without a pause, he bared his chest to the Sephian leader.

Apolo shook his head. "No, friend. I need you at full strength. I will take no more of your energy today. My wound is minor. I'll wait for a donor once I know the more seriously injured are secure."

In response, Legian gave him a hard look. He slowly fastened his shirt and soldiered up at Apolo's side. The colonel stood firm a few feet away.

As the leaders watched over them, Sienna turned her attention to watching the hallway turn into a makeshift hospital. Med-techs swabbed every injured soldier with the antitoxin before bandaging their wounds. Astonishingly, only Giphers had been killed, although several looked seriously injured. This wasn't over yet. Not by a long shot.

Sienna no longer felt pressure against her temple, and she looked up to see Jax watching her, his hand on the staff sergeant's gun, still inches from her head. After a tight nod from the major, the NCO backed off, slid the gun back into its holster, and helped Sommers to his feet.

A hand appeared in front of her and she grabbed it. Jax pulled her to her feet, saving her a lot of work, since her leg brace had been royally screwed up when she'd been knocked to the ground.

Jax motioned to the staff sergeant. "Ace, this is Gunny's widow. Don't point a gun at her again."

"Apologies, ma'am," Ace said. "Gunny was a good man."

"He was," she agreed as she leaned against the wall.

Without another word, the men moved. The major walked toward the leaders with Jax and Ace on either side. He paused to give her the bloodied bandana.

Apolo eyed the colonel, the *soullare* that vined around his eye making his gaze all the more intense. "I give you my word that I will get to the bottom of this outrage, and I promise you, justice will be both swift and merciless."

The officer, however, appeared less than swayed. "I have

no doubt, but how can you represent Sephians if you can't even control your own people?"

"If I may speak, sir?" Jax asked.

The officer nodded.

Jax spoke. "I have seen the enemy, sir. The Draeken are like nothing we've ever faced. I saw them kill over two hundred Sephians in minutes. What I saw will destroy us all if we don't stand together."

The colonel cocked his head. "If they are as vile as you say, why haven't they attacked us? Why have they only attacked Sephians?"

"Why haven't they attacked us until today, you mean? Look around you, sir. The Draeken have just declared war on the United States."

The officer glanced over the hallway and waved a hand in the air. "I saw no Draeken today. We have no proof. It could've been a mutiny by Apolo's own people."

"My people are loyal." Apolo stepped forward out of Legian's supporting arms. "I will get to the bottom of today's attack. Let's continue our discussion in my room."

Colonel Jerrick shook his head. "I think we've talked enough for one day."

Apolo's lips thinned. "It is my greatest hope that we can form an alliance... for the safety of your world."

The colonel watched Apolo for another second then nodded to Sommers, who in turn organized the soldiers. He then took a deep breath and looked around, his gaze settling on Jax. "Lieutenant, you remain here with your full platoon until further instructed. Report in to both Captain Fisher and Major Sommers at least three times per day."

"Yes, sir." Jax saluted and called out to his team.

"Apolo," Jerrick said. "I'm continuing to leave my men with you as an act of good faith. I expect you to ensure they are treated with the utmost respect, and receive open access to your base, people, information, and materials."

Apolo nodded. "You have my word. They will be given the same level of authority as my trinity." He paused and motioned to a Sephian couple, who stepped forward as though expecting to be called. "I would like to send two of my people with you for your questions, and I'm sure your doctors would like to better understand Sephian physiology. Sirlyn and Tejan are *tahren*—a bonded couple. As such, they are best equipped for you to learn about the key differences between Sephians and humans. And, I expect them to be treated as you expect your people to be treated here."

"Of course," the colonel replied.

Apolo continued. "In another act of good faith, I will not consider moving my base. You have our location. What you do with it will become a critical turning point in your world's history."

The colonel narrowed his eyes ever so slightly before giving a tight nod. "Until we talk again." Jerrick turned from Apolo and walked away surrounded by his soldiers, minus Jax's team of eight.

When Sienna felt the soldiers were a comfortable distance away, she rolled up her sleeves as she hobbled toward Apolo, who was now wavering on his feet. "Let's get you to the med-hub. And you better take some of our energy on the way." She leaned into him, trying to hold him up as Legian came to support both of them.

"That could've gone better," the Sephian leader muttered, his voice sounding weak.

Sienna blinked as Apolo drained her energy. "It will next time." And she hoped her words held true.

Chapter Twelve

So many thoughts swirled through Sienna's head as she sat in Apolo's room alongside Legian, Jax, and Nalea.

The door opened, and Sienna looked up to see a haggard Apolo enter the room. He now sported a fresh six-inch scar on his bicep, and a jagged line where a spur from the blood-charge must have slid across his arm rather than going straight in. Sienna had noticed the Sephians scarred more easily than their human counterparts and wondered if it had something to do with their accelerated healing abilities. Regardless of how fast a body healed, it still retained reminders. Instead of arthritis, the Sephians got scars.

Legian leaned forward, putting his elbows on the table. "Do you have an update on Bente?"

Some of Apolo's stress looked like it washed away with the question. "They got to him before he lost too much blood. When I checked in on him, he'd gone through three donors already and was onto a fourth. If his body accepts the new blood, he'll recover."

Nalea leaned back in her chair and looked up to the ceiling. "Praise the gods."

Legian nodded toward Apolo. "It looks like you could use another donor as well."

"We have more important business to discuss," Apolo replied with a sharp tone.

Legian gave his leader a disapproving look but, wisely, said nothing.

Apolo's fist knuckled the table. "After today's unfortunate incident, I believe it is safe to say that we remain on our own in our fight against the Draeken." He turned to Jax. "It isn't a lost cause; not yet. You and I will discuss how best to proceed tonight."

Jax nodded tightly.

"However, the alliance is not our immediate concern," Apolo continued. After a moment, he lowered his head and ran a hand through his long hair. "The Draeken influence is a festering wound in this base. Despite our best attempts, our comm-techs have found nothing. We are no closer today than we were before the ambush. We can no longer afford to wait for the traitor—or traitors—to make a mistake."

"You don't think Giphers did it," Legian said it in a way that sounded like he already knew the answer.

"That kid didn't have enough brains or balls for it," Nalea added.

"Any news from your spy?" Sienna asked.

Apolo frowned. "I lost contact with him immediately following the first base attack. Since the information he provided on the Draeken camp was faulty, I think it is safe to assume he has been compromised. We no longer have a viable source of information on the Draeken."

"*Suvaste*," Legian muttered.

Apolo nodded. "All the more reason to act now. Today's events made it clear. I believe the time has come to entice the *fregee* out of hiding." He rubbed his nearly healed arm and sat down. "Before he was compromised, my informant believed

Hillas died en route to Earth from injuries he sustained before he left Sephia."

Nalea leaned forward. "If Hillas is dead, Roden is in charge of all Draeken."

Legian scowled. "Unfortunately, we can't know that for sure. We don't know when your informant was compromised. They could have been feeding him misinformation longer than we realized."

Apolo shook his head. "Possibly, although I doubt it. He's too smart for that. The last communication I received from him was distorted and audio only, which I should have seen as a red flag. All we know for now is that we can no longer make assumptions about their military strategy."

From what Sienna had heard, Hillas, the all-powerful Draeken despot, was an in-your-face brutalist. The Draeken leader was a brilliant planner, but he had no respect for life. He'd charge right into battle with no thought as to casualties on either side.

Roden, on the other hand, was a wild card, thought to be insane. No one could figure out how he operated. He often avoided full frontal assaults, yet was known to be fond of sending soldiers on suicide missions. He served as one of Hillas's generals and was believed to be the only remaining high-ranking Draeken from the Noble War. Oh, and torture was his hobby.

Her leg throbbed at the thought of him.

"With Hillas, we knew what to expect. He's always operated with some sense of moral code. We cannot make such theories if Roden is now in command. Going forward, we will operate under the assumption that they may employ any strategy necessary," Apolo added. "Although we did gain one valuable piece of information today."

Sienna's eyes widened. "What's that?"

"The traitorous dog leaving its stench around this base is

on a Draeken leash. I am convinced the humans had no hand in either the ambush or the incident today. It narrows our scope considerably. The traitor is a Sephian with ties to the Draeken. Ties that have remained hidden to us. We will entice the traitor come to us."

Sienna winced. He'd thought the traitor could have been a human?

"To draw out the *fregee*, we need to offer something it cannot resist," Legian said.

Sienna tapped a finger to her lips as she thought. "How about letting it leak that the colonel shared the location of the Draeken core ship? That kind of intel should be irresistible to someone sympathetic to the Draeken."

Apolo tapped a forefinger to his lip. "We have kindling. Now we need a spark."

"Perhaps you conveniently keep the location and attack plans in your room," Legian added.

Apolo considered for a moment. "Yes. That should do it. We'll need to be careful about how we share this information. We don't want the traitor to become suspicious."

"My team can help with that," Jax said.

After another hour of planning, the group stepped out into the hall. The trap was ready to be set, and each person had a role to play. The traitor would be stopped tonight, no matter what.

Chapter Thirteen

It was a dull, recurring dance. Sit, stand, pace, sit again. Boredom threatened to overtake the group holed up in the tech-hub.

Bente was furious at Apolo for making him stay in the med-hub. His temper played into the plan perfectly, although Sienna felt sorry for the med-techs on duty. He'd proven to be the worst patient she'd ever seen. She'd picked up some new Sephian cuss words when they had restrained him, which must have been pretty colorful, since even Nalea refused to translate them for her.

The restraints wouldn't have held Bente if he'd really wanted out, so it was a good thing he'd obeyed his leader and remained there to play his part. Apolo had apprised Bente of the plan, which had only fueled Bente's anger at being bedridden during an important night.

On the down side, not having Bente in the room threw off the group's cadence. Even with the constant white noise of audio filtering in over the monitors across the base, the tech-hub was quieter without his quips, making the minutes drag. Her eyes glazed over while she stared at the dozen monitors on the wall, each of them showing different angles in Apolo's rooms and the hallways outside it.

If the information they had leaked made it to the right ears, Bente was miserably stuck in the med-hub—fact—while Apolo, Legian, and Nalea were to be off base tonight negotiating a new source for supplies—fiction.

The plan was beautiful in its simplicity. First, Legian and Nalea had grabbed a bite to eat at the Commons and told a few key people—the gossips—they were heading out tonight with Apolo. That kind of thing happened often, so the news was sure not to raise any red flags. Part one accomplished.

Two was where Jax's team came into play. Jax and his men had hit the training room during its busiest time to make sure they had plenty of company. After a half-hearted attempt at a work-out, they'd chatted about how Jax had got the okay to move into the officers' hall, converting the storage room next to Bente's into living space. They went into how it was great to hear some of the scoop first hand, such as the news of a bona fide Draeken base being found, and how Apolo was sitting on the news to play it safe.

To add a cherry on top, they had spilled that they were heading into town after Jax had moved his gear to his new room. It wouldn't take a scientist to figure out the officers' hall would be left empty, leaving only the tech-hub staffed. And the comm-techs were notorious for staying holed up in the room until their shifts were up.

The Sephians already had a disdainful view of human intelligence, so for Jax and his team to leak important information fit right into their preconceived stereotypes. With three hundred Sephians cooped up in an underground bunker, the news had likely zigzagged the entire base before they'd even left the training room. Aside from the continuously staffed tech-hub, this left the small officers' hallway vacant and ripe for the disreputable to pluck.

The plan had gone into effect three hours ago, when all the participants faked their departures then retreated to the tech-hub. Now it was a waiting game. What was going to happen, Sienna wasn't sure, but something *had* to happen. They'd been on the losing team too long. They needed this win.

With her feet propped up on the table, Sienna rocked her chair on two legs. It had never occurred to her before how boring security guards' jobs could be. Waiting, watching monitors, and waiting some more. No one spoke, except for Jax who checked in with his team every few minutes.

Sienna grabbed the bag of chips she'd brought and popped it open. She pulled out one chip and crunched it. Feeling like she was being watched, she looked up. Indeed, everyone in the room was staring at her. She held out the bag, and five palms raced out to meet her hand. She dumped out chips into the hands, and the room erupted in a chorus of crunches. Looking with disappointment at an empty bag a couple minutes later, she wished she'd brought a second bag. Now it was back to the waiting part.

"How's the leg?" Nalea asked her.

"Well, it's still attached. But I've discovered I could make a second career doing weather. My leg throbs every time it's going to rain." She shrugged. "Then again, it throbs every day."

"We have computers that track and forecast the weather for us," Tanel said. "They are one hundred percent accurate. I believe your leg cannot be as accurate."

"You'd be surprised," she muttered.

With no warning, the lights flickered on several screens, and then went out. Sienna hastily wiped her fingers across her jeans and glanced over at the wall of monitors. She frowned. Lights were still on across the base except in the vacant officers' hallway. Being underground as the base was, the hallway had no windows, leaving the screens pitch black. Even the nocturnal Sephians couldn't see in that kind of dark without some kind of help.

"We're blind," she spoke aloud. When she didn't get a response, she looked up at Apolo, who didn't look the least bit surprised. "You were expecting this?"

He nodded. "I suspected our prey may try this, and I had a taciturn system installed today in this hallway."

Seconds felt like minutes. Legian, Nalea and Jax scanned the monitors, and Sienna followed their lead. Tanel's fingers danced energetically across the digital keyboard. Then, a neon-outlined shape emerged on the screen. She had no idea what a taciturn system was, but it wasn't infrared. Whatever it was showed a lot more features and colors than any infrared image she'd seen before. She could see a man's shape, the outline detailed enough to show he was wearing some kind of goggles.

"And there is our prey," Apolo said to no one in particular.

Jax apprised his men through his earpiece. "Bravo Team, Tango has entered the box."

Everyone in the tech-hub watched in silence as the shape jogged down the hallway and stopped right outside Apolo's door. Sure enough, a moment later, after looking from side to side, the shape punched in a code and entered.

"Pull the bios on the intruder. When we get to my room, reset the power," Apolo commanded the comm-tech before turning to the two members of his trinity. "Let's go."

Apolo, Legian, and Nalea took the lead. Jax handed Sienna a flashlight, and Sienna grabbed her cane. She and Jax stepped in behind the trio, but Legian held out an arm, blocking them both.

"This is a Sephian matter. We need to resolve this."

Jax gave a nod and took a step back. "I'll have my team in the hallway on standby."

After the door closed, Sienna stepped up behind Tanel. His fingers ran across the flat keyboard, and the humanoid shape on the monitor to his left flashed as a string of symbols measured its shape and size and compared it against the stats of all the Sephians on the base. Names and pictures scrolled down the screen faster than she could follow.

She took off her *drades* and cleaned the lenses with the edge of her shirt. Sliding them back on, she turned her attention to the larger monitor in front and watched as three neon shapes moved down the hallway. She blew out a long breath. "They move like vampires."

"They have a history together. It shows," Jax answered.

"The bio information on the intruder is coming up now," Tanel announced into the hand-held mic as he continued to type on the console in front of him. "His name is Pilin. He's an op-tec, a level four operations engineer."

"A handyman. And not a very good one if he's only a level four," Sienna said, speaking out loud as much for her benefit as for Jax's.

Jax leaned closer to the screens. "It would take some skill to cut the power in just the officer's hall."

"And even more skill to cut the power and get to Apolo's room in under a minute."

"He's got a partner," they said in stereo.

Sienna thought for only a second. "Tanel, can you pull up the video feed near the power boxes just before the power went out?"

"It will take a couple minutes," Tanel replied.

Jax used his earpiece. "Bravo Team, possible second Tango in quadrant *tini*. Search for anyone who tickles your nose hairs."

Jax turned to Sienna and nodded. As they waited, Apolo's team reached the door to Apolo's rooms. He swiped his hand over the wall, and the door opened.

Apolo spoke some words in Sephian through the hand-held com. Tanel tapped several places on the keyboard at the same time, and the lights in the hallway came back on. Sienna and Jax watched as Legian and Nalea moved to stand alongside Apolo. The Sephian male was staring at the three like a deer caught in headlights now that the power was back on.

He tried to bolt, but Legian tackled him before he could take more than two steps toward the door. Apolo pulled the traitor to his feet and punched him. Even on the small screen, Sienna could see blood fly from the force of Apolo's hit. It was the angriest she'd ever seen him.

"I'm pulling up the video feed on monitor four now," Tanel said.

Sienna and Jax watched the video of an empty hallway. Several seconds into the feed, the screen became a blur.

Tanel pounded the screen. "*Suvaste*. They used a dampener."

"Can you clean up the image?" Jax asked.

The comm-tech shook his head. "No. I won't be able to identify anyone off this. Sorry."

The trio continued to watch the screen. The traitor was on his knees, whimpering as blood poured from his broken nose. His hands were banded behind his back. Nalea held a blaster to his head while she kept her other hand on his clothed shoulder. Sienna realized she was being careful to not come into direct contact, thus preventing Pilin from healing himself.

Legian stood back several feet and also had a blaster leveled on Pilin. Apolo was pacing back and forth in front of the prisoner, pausing long enough to glare at him midway through each lap. After a few more laps, he stopped before the kneeling Sephian and gave him a hard look. "How could you betray your own people?"

"Wha—what? I don't know what you're talking about."

The words were spoken in Sephian, and Sienna struggled to translate. "Tanel, turn on the translator."

Tanel tapped a couple commands. "There. I have the English translator on."

"Thanks," Sienna said as she watched the screen. On it, Apolo stared down at Pilin then kicked him in the gut. She cringed as the prisoner cried out then lost his lunch.

Oblivious to the mess, Apolo scowled and grabbed the man's collar. "How could you betray your own people?"

The prisoner coughed, fighting for breath. "I didn't. I swear it."

"You are a liar and a traitor. Your name will forever be a scar upon our people."

Tears ran down Pilin's face. He tried to get up, but Nalea knocked him back down.

"I remember you, Pilin. You have been in the detention block before. It was theft, if I recall. Oh, yes; you had stolen alcohol from the Commons. Is that how they got to you? Through your addiction?"

"I don't know what you're talking about. I am faithful to our people. I swear it."

"And, I suppose now you're telling me that breaking into my room is a simple misunderstanding?"

"Yes!"

Apolo didn't appear to like that answer, because he back-handed the Sephian across the face.

The prisoner cried out, "Please, please."

"You beg for mercy now? From the same people you sought to betray? Why would you betray your people, Pilin?"

He shook his head violently. "I would never betray our people."

Apolo slapped him. "I don't believe you. Every time I think you're lying, I will mark you. Do you understand?"

The man whimpered. Apolo nodded to Nalea, who bent Pilin's arms back in what had to be an unnatural position. The Sephian screamed in pain.

"Do you understand?"

"Yes!"

"Good. That's a start."

"Who do you work for, Pilin?"

"No one," he cried.

Apolo raised his hand and Pilin winced. The sound of the slap made Sienna wince in sympathy pain. *Tell the truth, man.*

"I'm going to ask you one more time. Who do you work for?"

Pilin's shoulders shook from his uncontrollable sobs. "I swear, Apolo. I came here for a bottle of whiskey. I heard you kept the good stuff here. That's all. I swear it."

Apolo lifted his hand, and Pilin let out a yelp. But Apolo didn't slap him this time; instead, he bent down to come eye to eye with the prisoner. "Who told you that, son?"

He shook his head with his sobs. "It was a rumor I heard at the Commons."

"And who cut the power?"

"I—I don't know. The engineering log showed a power test was scheduled to be conducted in the officers' hall at ten o'clock. That's what it said. Precisely ten o'clock. I grabbed night gear just in case. I thought it was a lucky break. That's all."

Apolo grabbed Pilin's chin who yelped. "You know the punishment for treason, Pilin?"

The poor man looked up with a look of shock. "Tr —treason?"

"Yes, treason. What you did tonight, regardless of intentions, was treason. Tell me. Who sent you here?"

He sobbed. "No one. I swear it," he stammered before breaking down into an uncontrollable crying fit.

Apolo came to his feet. "Sephian law states the punishment for treason is immediate death, Pilin. I will make yours swift out of pity because you were played the fool."

In a blur of movement, Apolo grabbed and twisted the man's head. A loud crack broke the silence. Sienna inhaled sharply, covering her mouth with the back of her hand. She'd never seen an execution before.

At that moment, she was glad she was leaning against the comm-tech's desk. Otherwise, she was sure her knees would have given out. She couldn't take her eyes off the man now lying on the floor, his neck bent at an unnatural angle. She didn't even hear Jax move until a hand touched her shoulder.

She jumped.

He brushed a hand down her cheek. "You okay?"

The question sounded more like a command, and she nodded with as much confidence as she could muster. "I'm fine."

He stayed at her side while she continued to watch. No one in the room seemed fazed by what Apolo had done. They all watched Apolo, unmoving, as he stared at the wall, his mind obviously somewhere else.

"How will we know who gave him the information?" Legian asked.

Apolo answered instead. "That was the one thing he could never tell us. He didn't know. He was simply a pawn. There was nothing else we could have learned from him." The look on Apolo's pained face betrayed his strong voice. "The traitor knows that we tried to trap him."

"How so?" Nalea asked.

"Pilin came here looking for whiskey, not for information," Apolo said.

Legian frowned. "Pilin was set up to fail. But why?"

Apolo answered. "Pilin must have known who the traitor

is, even if he wasn't aware that he knew. He'd likely been used by the traitor before without knowing."

Apolo paused to speak to Tanel. "Pull everything you have on Pilin in the week before and after the base attack, as well as today's attack. Search everything. Make a list of every single Sephian he came into contact with and every single activity he did—no matter how small. If he defecated, I want to know. Do you understand?"

Tanel spoke so fast in Sephian that Sienna couldn't make out the words.

Apolo turned back to look down at the dead man. "Sending the drunk here would be an easy way to clean up loose ends. The traitor would know there is no leeway in dealing with treason. We're too low in numbers. The disappearance of any Sephian would be noticed quickly."

Nalea spoke. "If the traitor is cleaning house, it could mean he thinks he has something all ready to go."

Apolo nodded tightly. "Or, he's found a new pawn to use. I believe it's time for us to make the next move."

Chapter Fourteen

"Do you yield?" Legian boomed.

"Never," Sienna shoved out through clenched teeth while she knelt on her hands and knees, panting. The pain in her leg was agonizing. She'd always had some cellulite, but now she felt like a jellyfish. This session felt worse than her first one. She was weak and hurting. And the worst part? Legian knew it.

Her sparring partner held out a hand, his face tight. "Yield, Sienna. Please."

She slapped his hand away.

Moving about as fast as a snail through peanut butter, she pulled herself up, trying not to favor her bad leg. It burned like acid with each movement. She grunted through the pain and somehow managed to get to her feet. Legian gave her space while she came to her full height across from him on the training mats.

She knew what she looked like. She'd been getting her ass handed to her all morning. She looked around the massive training room as she took the time to catch her breath. Padded sparring rings covered the floor, each a different color.

Weapons of various shapes and sizes filled racks lined against the dark walls. A muted sound from the filtration system filled the air, like white noise, only less obtrusive. More like a gentle sigh.

Today, they used no weapons, instead working on fundamentals. Her leg couldn't support her own weight, let alone any sharp moves. She wore a stiff brace, and even with it she could barely stand. Without it, she was crippled.

But she would do this. She had to do this. She motioned to Legian. "Again."

He raised an eyebrow and stared at her. When he realized she was serious, he gave a proud smile... then he attacked. His arm shot out, and she dodged to the left. He kicked out a leg, and she jumped. She landed with a wince, but that wasn't what pissed her off.

"You're holding back," she snarled when a blow rolled off her shoulder.

"You're injured," he said, matter-of-factly.

"Doesn't matter. I could be injured during a battle and would still need to fight."

He stepped back. "You sure about this?"

"Sure as your skin sparkles, Tinkerbell."

He narrowed his eyes while he examined her for a moment before he shrugged and attacked. This time for real; she was flat on her back in under a second.

Sienna embraced the pain. Turning it into a war-scream, she twisted and grabbed Legian's legs in a double-takedown maneuver. Except he didn't go down. Just as she'd planned. She switched her pressure, pulling back rather than pushing. It knocked him off balance, and he fell toward her.

She twisted on the ground in time to keep him from toppling onto her, but he ducked his chin and rolled head-first to the side. He was on his feet and attacking before she was standing. Diving to the left, she narrowly missed his swing. He snapped around. She held her breath and leapt at him. He moved to the right like she expected, and she spun her good leg out the moment she hit the ground. She knocked him off balance and fell on him.

With a full-out smile, she looked down to a surprised Legian.

"Do you yield?" Sienna asked in her best smart-ass tone as she straddled him.

He looked up with a wide grin, and her smile dropped.

Suddenly, she was the one with her back to the mat, staring up at the lights. "Dammit. Not again."

"I was having too much fun seeing the look of success in your eyes. You actually thought you had me," he replied, standing victor over her.

"How's training going?"

She looked up to see Apolo saunter into the training room.

Legian turned to face Apolo. "Sienna's doing good for a human. She'll be in prime condition in no time."

Apolo walked around Legian and bent down, leaning his forearm on one knee no more than a foot or so from her. She pulled herself to one elbow and looked him in the eye. She refused to cower under intimidation, and she wanted to make sure he knew it. "But the real question is will your leg be a weakness we can afford out there?"

"I won't be weak," Sienna said.

He backed away. "Show me that your leg won't be a detriment."

Legian stepped forward. "She's not ready."

"She's a human *and* the *tahren* of one of my trinity. As such, she will be at the forefront of sensitive negotiations. We don't have the luxury of waiting for her to be ready," the Sephian leader said.

Legian lowered his head and stepped off the mat. Sienna eyed him, and he looked at her, tense, unmoving.

Apolo motioned her to him. "Any time you're ready, human." He didn't even widen his stance. He assumed she was harmless.

She turned her pain into rage and launched at him. He didn't bother to move out of the way. Instead, he held his arms out and embraced her as she rammed into him. She dropped and swept out his legs. Apolo fell to the floor with a look of surprise, as if he hadn't expected her to take him down. She took advantage of his hesitation and clapped her hands on his sensitive ears.

That pissed him off. In the next second, she found herself slammed against the mat so hard she could have sworn a tooth got knocked loose, a knee against her throat. She clawed at his leg. He watched her gasp for air, smiled, and the weight was gone. She grabbed the hand in front of her, and Apolo pulled her to her feet. The brace clanked as her leg straightened, pulling her healing muscles too tight. She bit her lips to keep from flinching.

Apolo showed her no mercy because she was female. He held true to the Sephian belief that females were as strong as their male counterparts. A belief Sienna firmly supported, although right now she was feeling markedly less than anyone's equal.

She turned to face him, taking in shallow breaths while he scrutinized her. After a moment, he gave her a slight tilt of his head, like he approved. Of what, she had no idea. Apolo nodded at Legian. "Continue with training," he said and walked out.

The moment he left, she collapsed back to the floor and inhaled sharply. Her eyes burned from sweat. She yanked off her bandana, wiped off her face, and tied it back around her wrist. With a quick tug, she tightened her ponytail then fell to her back. She could feel Legian sit down next to her as she stared at the ceiling.

"Apolo is our greatest warrior," Legian said. "There's no shame in losing to him."

She grunted. "Why did he lead the Sephian force here? There has to be so much that he could do back on Sephia."

"Krysea asked him to lead us here. I would follow him to my death, as would any other Sephian. Other than Krysea, there are no other Sephians who command such respect."

She shook her head. "I get why she asked him, but, I mean, why did he accept?"

"He would never turn down an assignment Krysea gave him. Our leader has always done what's best for our people. He knows that and accepts it."

"Yeah, but what about what's best for her? For Apolo?"

Legian brought himself up on an elbow and ran a hand over her skin. "That's not her way. Or his, for that matter."

She bent her leg slowly until the muscles released.

"Your leg needs rest. Why don't we stop for today?"

Her lips thinned. "And if my leg never heals?"

"Human healing takes time. Take it one step at a time."

"But what if?"

Legian frowned like he didn't understand.

"What if I never heal? Apolo's right. He can't afford any sign of weakness."

"Sienna, I would love it if you never stepped foot in combat. I raced to find you when I heard the base was attacked. You are many things, but you have never been weak."

She took hold of each of his hands and he helped her to her feet. She gave him a soft kiss. He went to embrace her, but she turned away. She hobbled over to the weapons rack and grabbed a long wooden stick and twirled it in her hand.

"Again."

Chapter Fifteen

Nalea motioned Legian and Sienna into the room. Bente, Jax, and Apolo were already there, sitting around the black table and looking down at a screen that covered nearly the entire flat surface. Standing behind Jax were three of his team, who Sienna knew only by their last names: Hurt, Quincy, and White.

She pushed the *drades* up her nose before she hobbled into the room, using her cane for support. Legian closed and locked the door behind them. No one else looked up when they entered. They were too absorbed with whatever was on the screen, mumbling as they hunched over the table.

Legian pulled a chair out for Sienna and she sat down, hanging the cane by its handle on the back of the chair. He took the seat next to her. Her eyes were drawn to the image on the screen. It was a detailed 3-D floor plan of what looked to be a large office building or warehouse. It was colored differently than any floor plan she'd seen, but the outline was the same. Sections were filled in with bright colors. Chartreuse for hallways, fuchsia for the open area. It was like seeing a rainbow for the first time. Beautiful, yet every color had its place.

The image looked so real, she fought back the urge to reach out and touch it. Sephians had the coolest technology. Actually, it was Draeken technology, since the Sephians had been nothing more than their worker bees for a couple centuries. Designed by Draeken, built by Sephians. It made for a nice sense of irony that the slaves had used their masters' technology to gain their freedom.

And use it the Sephians did. The base was filled with technology adapted to their needs. They were experts at survival, and adjusting to other cultures seemed a tool of the trade. Since she had come on the base, she'd begun to see familiar objects pop up everywhere, from video games to guns, and laptops to magazines. The Sephians were starved for anything they could get their hands on. She figured it had something to do with growing up in slavery. There wasn't a Sephian on this base who had owned much of anything before they broke free from Draeken control. Some, like Legian, maintained a minimalist attitude, while many others turned into pack rats.

Sienna wanted to spend more time pondering what made the Sephians tick, but there were more important things at hand. She leaned back in her seat and made eye contact with Apolo. "What am I looking at here?"

Apolo shot her a quick look before his eyes dropped to his wrist computer, which reminded her of a wide smart watch with metallic straps. He hit a series of buttons, and a strange silver glow with a muted vibration fell over the room. It seemed to come from nowhere and everywhere at the same time.

"Dampener device," Apolo said in Jax's direction. "It prevents any type of audio from being tapped from this room."

Squinting, Sienna examined the walls and ceilings for some small contraption, but she couldn't find the source.

Apolo gestured over the image. "What you see before you is the last piece of viable intel I received from my Draeken informant before he went silent."

Sienna narrowed her eyes, waiting for Apolo to continue. He didn't, so she spoke up. "How do we know we can trust that what your inside guy gave us was any good? They could have gotten to him long before the base attack."

Apolo's attention snapped to her. "This intel came in two weeks before the ambush, and came through with visual and audio unlike the faulty intel we received later." Suddenly, he hit the table with his fist, causing the image to shiver. Everyone froze in their chairs while he clenched his fists. Apolo's moods were worsening, and rumors were spreading that he may eventually lose his mind after being separated from his *tahren* for so long. The odds weren't in his favor.

The plastic-like material ended up with a perfect knuckle-sized indentation before slowly regaining its original smoothness. When Apolo finally continued, he didn't look up. "I should have known better than to trust that intel. Instead, I grabbed onto an opportunity that seemed too good to pass up. The chance to stop the Draeken in one fell swoop. Someone played me for a fool." He clenched and unclenched his fists as he spoke. "The intel that led us into the attack on the base was the last communication I received from him. Before that, he reported in multiple times a month."

He paused and glanced at each face around the table. "This data, although incomplete, is good; I'm sure of it. I have been holding on to it until my informant could send more information. At this point, we know he's gone silent or has been compromised, and so I must assume we will be unable to collect more data."

"If they got to your informant, it makes sense that's how

they found the location of our base," Bente added, softening his usual brusque tone.

Apolo shook his head. "Impossible. My man does not know the location of this base. He is nearly unbreakable—"

Bente raised a finger.

Apolo replied to Bente's unvoiced interruption by patting down the air with his hands. "Yes, I know everyone can be broken. That was why I ensured my informant knew nothing of our base location. It's safe to assume we have our traitor to thank for leaking the location of the base to the Draeken. If only my informant wasn't so protective of his own people and had shared the location of the Draeken camp before..."

Apolo came to his feet, clasped his hands behind his back, and walked around the table. Everyone sat in silence and watched the leader pace. He was seemingly oblivious to anyone else in the room. On his third time around the table, he paused and pointed at the image. "We need to focus on what we can control. So far, we have nothing more besides this floor plan and a partial address."

His fingers brushed over the image, and the screen zoomed in on a section of rooms. "Bente, you've spent more time in Draeken facilities than any of us. Look closely at this block of rooms. My informant believed this to be the location of something along the lines of a Draeken-human interaction center.

"After looking at the floor plan, we believe it may be a medical center. A human breeding facility, to be exact."

Sienna shoved her chair back from the table in a rush. "Human breeding? You can't mean..." Her voice trailed off.

Apolo nodded tightly. "Yes. I do. We know the Draeken female population was decimated in the Noble War. Their numbers are desperately low. It makes sense that they are pursuing the survival of their race through cross-breeding. In fact, we believe this may be the primary reason they chose this planet. As we've discovered ourselves recently,"—Apolo waved a hand in Legian's and her general direction—"humans are genetically compatible with our race. There's no reason not to believe it is also the case for the Draeken."

"It's like a bad sci-fi movie," Quincy said from behind Jax.

"Yeah," Smith added. "Not only do they want our world, but they want our women? No effing way."

"That's assuming they're willing to stoop that low and taint their Draeken bloodlines," Bente added from the side.

"If their numbers are low enough, they can't afford pride," Jax retorted.

Bente scowled. "You sure this is a medical facility? It's not laid out like one." He went back to looking at the screen. His eyes narrowed, and then he pointed at a long hallway with a series of rooms on the screen. "This area looks suspicious."

"My informant couldn't confirm its use," Apolo said, "but he was confident it was neither a military installation nor a place that brought harm to humans. He advised me of the location with the intention that I avoid it rather than go after it."

"We're going in, aren't we?"

"Yes," Apolo said.

Nalea pointed to the same area of the floor plan that Bente had noted. "This area should be our primary target. Outside of the larger area, all the smaller rooms attach to this hallway. It's the hub. Most of their medical equipment and prisoners are likely to be contained here."

"Is there any way we can verify what your informant said is true?" Sienna asked.

Bente leaned forward stiffly and examined the image. "Recon."

"Do we know if they're drawing the human women to this location, or are they capturing them then bringing them there?" Legian asked.

"We believe they are being drawn there. Tanel researched the location and said that this large room is used as an entertainment venue." Apolo's fingers brushed over the display he wore on his forearm. He paused to read it. "It's called Mayhem. Tanel says it's called a 'Goth' club. He's researching it further now."

"That means it's a night club where folks in dark clothes get together to hang out, dance, drink, and what not," Sienna explained.

Jax nodded. "It would be easy to drug women's drinks in a dark bar."

She jerked at the truth in his words. The idea of drugging someone pissed her off. It was one thing to fight someone face to face, but taking advantage of someone like that was dishonorable. "You're right. They probably use something like roofies. From there, they could restrain the poor girls throughout the pregnancy." She fidgeted with the bandana on her wrist as she spoke.

"But the simplest plan would be to let the girls go," White continued. "They wouldn't even need to keep their victims more than a couple hours. Just long enough to tag 'em and bag 'em. The girls would never know what hit them. Basically, it would be a breed-and-release program. If they picked carefully, the girls would think they got knocked up during a one-night stand. The Draeken could sit back and wait until their nine months were up then go in and take the infants."

Sienna leaned back and shook her head. "That's wrong in so many ways."

"I think the victims would catch on when ultrasounds showed extra appendages," Jax added on.

Legian wrapped an arm around Sienna. He did that whenever he was stressed. And with a clenched jaw, he was definitely looking stressed. "Hybrids likely wouldn't develop wings, but we can't know for sure. They likely restrain the victims."

"We can get intel from a distance to see the amount of traffic the place gets, but we'd need to get up close and personal to know for sure," Nalea said.

Sienna glanced up at her friend. She hadn't noticed how Nalea had nearly lost her Sephian accent. Before long, she'd be like any other American. Well, except the golden skin and black eyes. That would still be a bit of a problem. Contacts would hide the eyes, but there was no realistic makeup to do the trick to their skin.

Apolo nodded. "We need to get an inside look." He looked from Jax to Sienna. Legian's grip tightened on her shoulder. "Jax's team and Sienna will be our scouts. Jax and Sienna will enter the club as a pair, with Bravo Team armed and ready outside. We need to verify the Draeken have set up a facility."

Jax used his fingers to move through the floor plan. Even with this being his first time using the technology, he operated it like a pro. "We need to know what we're looking for, as well as their usual security measures."

Nalea rubbed her neck. "Trust me. You'll know. While Draeken technology is far more advanced than human technology, it is also noticeable. I can show you common equipment to look for. As for security, assume the worst."

Bente looked Sienna up and down, and she frowned at him. He frowned back. "If it is a Draeken facility, they will have surveillance throughout and around the building. It will be critical to blend in. You do not look like the usual clientele."

"And Roden's seen her before. If they have any kind of professional op going on, we'll be busted before we walk through the door," Jax chimed in. "Sienna should stay behind. My team can handle this."

Sienna held up a finger. "First, with some hair color and makeup, my own mother wouldn't recognize me." She held up a second finger. "And nine tough guys walking into a Goth club will look a hell of a lot more suspicious than a couple."

"But with a shit leg, you still put the mission at risk."

She narrowed her eyes at Bente, aka Mr. Pessimist. "Doc has been working up a new brace for my leg. He thought he could have it ready by tomorrow. I'll be able to go without a cane. He says I might not even have a limp when I wear it. Besides, I'll have Jax with me. He's trained for this sort of thing. He's a super commando."

"Special Operations," Jax corrected.

"Sienna's going in," Apolo said. "If this is a breeding facility, a human woman will help Jax gain access to the club. A single man, let alone multiple single men, may not be able to enter the club without drawing notice." Whatever he typed next caused the screen to go blank. "We'll have analysis back from the comm-tech by tomorrow. We'll reconvene after second meal to finalize preparations. In the meantime, get some rest. You'll need it."

Then he tapped out a few more keystrokes. The lights switched back to normal and the mild vibration disappeared. Apolo exited through the door to his bedroom without another word. Everyone stood—Bente taking as long as Sienna to get to his feet—then left, Legian and Sienna silently following the others out of the room.

Going deep into Draeken territory terrified her, but she wasn't going to complain. Hell, she was finally getting a chance to make a difference.

There was no way she'd let her new people down.

Chapter Sixteen

J ax pulled the car to a stop, and then looked over at her. "I'm impressed, Sienna. You'll fit in perfect."

"You clean up pretty decent yourself." In fact, Sienna was surprised at how well Jax Gothed up. They had used matching deep red and black hair color, and he'd even let her use kohl eyeliner on him. He wore black leather pants, motorcycle boots, and a tight black tee.

She, on the other hand, was dressed all in black, from the leather strapless corset over a black satin shirt to the full-length skirt hiding her new leg brace.

A hodgepodge of black plastic-like straps, the brace looked more like some kind of bondage toy than a medical device—oddly appropriate. The kinetic bands harvested energy from her body, which was then converted into power for the brace. She didn't even limp, let alone feel much pain, with the brace; it was an extension of her body.

The cane was now unnecessary, but she'd kept it anyway, hanging it on her wall to remind her of the risks she'd faced.

A valet opened the car door, held out his gloved hand, and helped her out of the car. Her steel-toed black leather boots made a solid thump on the sidewalk. She then waited at the curb.

Jax walked around the car and held out an arm, which she looped her hand through. His nose ring caught the light as he watched her, like he was measuring how badly she was going to screw up. "Ready to do this?"

"I have a knife in each boot, a gun tucked into my garter, a tracker in my corset, and I'm wearing an earpiece. I think I'm ready."

Sienna could barely hear Legian's warning to be careful in her ear over the bass radiating from the club. She stayed on Jax's arm as they approached the front door. Jax handed the doorman a couple of large bills. The man unhooked a red rope and they stepped under the neon *Mayhem* sign written in dripping blood-red letters. They strolled past two more large doormen then down a long, dark hallway that opened up onto a huge ballroom. Everything was exactly as the floor plan had shown.

So far, so good.

It was Sienna's first time in a Goth club, and she took in the decadent scenery. Tall crimson velvet curtains were draped down the twenty-foot black walls. Deep red couches and dark cherry tables were scattered across a floor packed wall-to-wall with dark-haired, dark-dressed people.

Some people lounged on the couches, drinking, talking, making out, and all combinations of those things. Many more were on the dance floor, gyrating to rave music with a bold, dark beat. Looking down from the top of the stairs, the dance floor reminded her of a subdued mosh pit. She felt herself swaying to the haunting, almost drug-like beat that vibrated through her body.

Jax nuzzled her ear with his nose. "Don't stare. This is our kind of place, remember?"

She closed her eyes and inhaled the cool air, which

contained a hint of incense. "Just getting the vibe of the place." She put a painted fingernail to her lips. "I wonder if the guards at the door are to keep folks out or to keep folks in."

Jax's lips tightened, and he didn't look like he was entirely sure himself.

"C'mon," she said, leading him toward the stairs. "Let's get a drink."

With a nod, he took the lead, sweeping her down the wide stairs and straight to the bar. The bartender gave Sienna a full-body once-over look. Whatever he saw must have satisfied him because he leaned closer with a flirty grin. "What will you have, sweets?"

"I'll have a tawny port. Aged twenty-years, preferably," she said, licking her lips under a flirty gaze.

He winked at her, and then turned a cool appraisal onto Jax.

"Templeton Rye on the rocks."

The bartender nodded and went about getting their drinks while Sienna swayed in time to music that would leave her ears ringing for days.

A glint of metal caught her eye. She glanced over at a girl with a dozen piercings. Dressed in a micro-mini leather skirt and strapless corset covered in a skull print, she fit right in with the crowd. What kept Sienna's attention, however, was the tattoo that spanned the girl's shoulder. It was of an angel in flight. Only this angel's wings didn't have feathers. Instead, its dragon-like wings were covered in tattoos.

Sienna eyed Jax, and he gave a glance that told her he was thinking the same thing. She nudged the petite girl. "Wicked ink."

The girl grinned and glanced over her shoulder as though she could see the tattoo. "Thanks. Got it done last week."

"Haven't seen a demon done like that before. With all the marks and stuff."

"I know. Isn't he sexy? His name is Laze. He takes the best care of me. And he is incredible." She said the last word with an over-exaggerated bend of her knees.

Sienna batted playfully at her. "No way. You met a real demon? Get outta here."

She rolled her eyes. "You're new here, aren't you?"

"New in town."

The girl nodded. "Hang out here long enough, maybe you'll see for yourself."

Sienna must have looked doubtful because the girl grabbed Sienna by her arms and looked her in the eye. "At first, they come to you when the fog machines smoke up the place. It's so surreal, it could be a dream. Only it's not a dream. And the things they do to you…" She shivered before playfully running a finger down Sienna's neck, sending sensual goosebumps across her skin. The girl smiled. "You're a bit old, but you're hot. Maybe you'll find out for yourself. After all, they need us," she whispered with a brush of her lips against Sienna's ear.

Sienna cocked her head. "Need us?"

Tat-girl gave her a knowing smile. "You'll find out if you're chosen. Trust me, you would never have to worry about money or anything ever again. That's how good they take care of us."

The girl was probably already pregnant by her demon lover and didn't even know it yet. Sienna made a mental note of the name Laze.

When Sienna opened her mouth to speak, Jax handed her the sipper of wine, and then wrapped an arm around her waist. Jax gave the other girl a flirty half-smile. "If you don't mind, I need this woman to myself."

With that, he tugged Sienna forward.

Jax put a hand on her hip and Sienna led the way to an open sofa near the wall. Old-fashioned drop-lights hung from the ceiling, shedding just enough yellowish light that she didn't trip over anyone. She'd become decent over the past few months at not crashing into things in the dark. Moving around this club was a piece of cake compared to getting around the base without her *drades*.

The leather corset creaked against the leather sofa as she sat down and propped her boots up on the coffee table, crossing her ankles. Jax sat next to her, wrapping an arm around her. To anyone else, they looked like any other hot-and-heavy couple watching the scene.

"Why the rush?" Sienna asked. "I was getting good intel at the bar."

"The bartender was beginning to eye you like you were a news reporter," Jax replied before narrowing his eyes in concentration.

"Oh."

Static sounded through her earpiece, but she couldn't make out any words. Taking the smallest sip of wine, she did her best to fit in while listening for more to come out through her earpiece.

"Repeat last." Jax spoke to her, although she knew he wasn't talking to her.

Again, a garbled response came through her earpiece.

"No joy," Jax replied with a frown and eyed Sienna. "Looks like we're on our own in here."

"At least the cavalry is just outside."

"A lot can happen in a couple hundred feet." He leaned back, resting an arm over the back of the couch. He watched the crowd for several moments before speaking again. "Things are a mess right now."

"Not everything," Sienna said. "From what I hear, you and Risa are hitting it off."

He thought for a moment. "I don't know what the fuck I'm doing."

"I know that feeling," she said.

"At least Doc's no longer an issue."

Sienna frowned, then her eyes widened. "Oh, I thought Doc just liked to flirt with her."

Jax shook his head. "There was more than flirting going on. And I got tired of that shit fast."

"How long did you know?"

He turned back to her and raised an eyebrow.

"Yeah. I guess you probably knew from the get-go. The base is small. And you are a super commando type." She put a hand on his knee. "Well, I'm glad she got her act together. You could use some fun in your life."

Jax replied by taking a drink of his whiskey.

Sienna looked back toward the bar. "This club is a perfect setting for the Draeken to meet women. I don't think it's a breeding facility in the way it sounded. It sounds more like a way for the Draeken to introduce themselves to humans who'd be accepting of them in the right atmosphere. Pretty brilliant plan if you ask me. That girl sounded like a pretty satisfied customer."

"Could be, but if they're worried about extinction, I wouldn't be surprised if they don't have more going on." Jax nodded and stared off into the crowd, running a hand up and down Sienna's arm while he scanned the club. He had one leg crossed over the other. Even though she knew he felt otherwise, he looked right at home. He handled himself so well she couldn't help but relax against him.

She had become entranced by an androgynous couple on the dance floor when a waitress with way too much eyeliner stepped into her line of sight.

"Can I get you two anything?"

"We're good." Jax brushed her off, and the waitress moved on to the next table without so much as a smile.

Sienna rested her head on his shoulder and glanced across the dance floor. "I don't see any doors, so I'm thinking they must be hidden behind these curtains."

"That's my thought, too."

She closed her eyes and rubbed her temple as she struggled to recall the exact floor plan. This was one of those times when a photographic memory would come in handy. To their left was the hallway to the restrooms. From there, the entrance above. She looked to the right. Directly behind the dance floor. There. It had to be there.

"The door is behind the second curtain on that wall."

"Playing The Price is Right?" Jax asked with a raised eyebrow.

She gave him a look of frustration. "See how the light is burned out above that one. It's the only light not working in this whole place. I bet it's intentional. It's so dark, it would be impossible to see someone coming and going."

He casually scanned the club before standing and holding out a hand. "Let's dance."

After a quick perusal of the crowded floor, she placed her hand in his. They weaved through the tables between them and the dance floor. When they reached the crowded dance floor, Jax pulled her hand above her head and gave her a twirl.

"Déjà vu," she said. "Minus the cowboy hat. What did you ever do with that? I liked it."

He smiled and gave her another twirl. "No one said we can't have a little fun while working."

Sienna laughed. It felt good. She couldn't remember the last time she had a full, real laugh. Lately, there hadn't been a lot to laugh at.

The song switched over, and the crowd migrated to the dance floor.

"I can't believe I know this song!" she yelled into his ear over the noise.

"I'm going to dance you toward the wall."

Jax steered them charmingly through the sea of slowly gyrating bodies and toward the edge of the dance floor. The room was beginning to swim when Jax stopped abruptly. Her head hit his chest.

"I'll cover you while you check the curtain."

He gave Sienna the lightest push, but her left leg missed a step and she torpedoed toward the wall. She stopped herself from meeting the wall face first and turned around. Jax was nowhere to be found. Tightening her lips, she dove behind the curtain, and, sure enough, there was a large steel door with no handle, only a flat electronic screen on the wall.

She backed up to tell Jax, but a large body blocked her.

"Ah!"

Jax held her steady. "Shh."

She poked him in the chest, accentuating each word. "Don't scare me like that. What are you trying to do? Give a girl a heart attack?"

He ignored her, and instead leaned her against the wall and stepped up to the screen.

"Apolo gave us a direct order to not do anything to raise suspicion," she said when she saw him pull out a small pen-like device.

"We can't get intel unless we take some risk," he replied, and raised the device to the screen.

She crossed her fingers. The comm-tech had sworn the thing would work and was one-of-a-kind. He'd also went on and on about it being worth more than Jax and her combined, but she liked to think Tanel was being a touch overprotective of his gadgets. Then again, knowing the Sephian's complete lack of any sense of humor, maybe not.

A light flashed on the screen, and the door opened with a whoosh.

"You good?" he asked.

She hiked up her skirt and pulled out her gun. "Let's do this."

From the other side of the doorway, Jax held up three fingers, then two, then one.

Show time.

They stepped through the door and into a brightly-lit room. She swung her gun around, her back to Jax, as they scanned the empty room. After a full three-sixty, she lowered her gun. A row of kegs lined one wall, while the others were lined with boxes of liquor.

She didn't know what she'd expected, but this wasn't it. "Do you think they got to Apolo's spy earlier than Apolo thought?"

"Maybe. Maybe the intel was bad. From the looks of things, they could've closed down months ago—if they were even here."

Sienna shook her head. "No way. That girl's ink was brand new. Something's off." She did another full turn to take in the room. "Wait a sec. In the floor plan, this room was longer than this."

Jax scanned the walls then walked to the far end of the room and began pulling boxes out. She followed suit. After moving a couple dozen cases, she froze. "I found something."

At that moment, something metallic clinked them. She glanced down at the object. "Chaos-charge! Cover your—"

Too late. The thing must have been on a short timer; the room erupted in light and screaming. She fell like a leaf in a tornado of bright light and noise.

"Legian!" she screamed, even though she knew he probably couldn't hear her. She could faintly hear Jax's yell for backup.

She rolled over and was trying to figure out which way was up when something grabbed her hand. Or, more precisely, something grabbed the gun from her hand while a tremendous pressure held her down. She tried to slap away her assailant, but with the vertigo, her hands wouldn't listen to her brain and she pretty much lay there, useless, as she was disarmed. She listened to the clinks of knives and charges being dropped onto the floor. Her weapons.

"Bastard," Sienna muttered, and a deep chuckle broke the now painful ringing silence in her ears. She wouldn't be surprised if both eardrums had burst, given the way they throbbed and the ringing that had set up in her ears. She looked around, taking several moments for the room to quit spinning. After what seemed like forever, her eyes slowly focused on the shape of a seven-foot Draeken standing over her. Her head jerked around as she searched for Jax, and she found him prone on the floor alongside her.

She jerked up, only to have a large hand shove her back onto the floor. She hadn't seen the other Draeken that knelt by her. She struggled against him, but he held her down with one hand, seemingly without effort.

She recalled the tattoo she'd seen earlier and recognized the wings. "You must be Laze."

He raised an eyebrow. "Come here to find me, did you?"

The Draeken next to him chuckled. "Your reputation precedes you. Perhaps she wants to experience a real man."

Sienna renewed her struggles. "I'd rather eat a forty-five than touch you."

"Spunk. I like that. But you're not my type. You smell of slaves." Laze's eyes narrowed. "How did you find us?"

"The Yellow Pages."

124

Laze grabbed her jaw and she winced. "I don't like to repeat myself. How did you find us?"

"She doesn't know anything. She came with me," Jax called out from several feet away.

She heard the sound of a punch, followed by a grunt. She couldn't turn her head toward the sound. She could only look up or close her eyes. And there was no way in hell she was going to let the Draeken think she was scared of him. She watched him turn toward Jax and grin. "Relax, human. We'll get to you soon enough." The devious smile was turned back onto her. "You will both tell me what you know. That, I promise."

She struggled harder, and he laughed. Then a loud sound cut the air, and warm liquid splattered her face. The Draeken fell like a heavy wall on her, and she fought to get out from under him, unable to breathe.

As quickly as it happened, the weight was gone, and she gulped fresh air. Legian fell to his knees and pulled her from the Draeken.

"Glad you could make it," she said, with as much humor as she could muster.

Legian bent down and kissed her then pulled away. "Let's get you out of here."

"Sounds good to me. After we finish checking this place out."

He helped her to her feet, only to throw her toward the wall again. A laser shot whizzed by her head. Coming to her hands and knees, she turned to see Legian reach for his gun. "Get out of here. *Run.*"

Chapter Seventeen

ike hell I'm leaving you.

L That was Sienna's first thought when shots fired from the now-open door that'd been hidden behind crates in the far wall. Both Legian and Nalea—who'd come in with Legian, Jax's team, and a couple other Sephians—were directly in the line of fire.

He fired a couple shots at the doorway. "Go outside! There's a dampener in this building. Our coms don't work. Call Apolo for backup."

He turned his attention back to the battle. She ran a couple steps and crashed into the fallen Draeken—Laze— who moaned. She turned to see Legian pop off more shots, but then he shot a look right back to her. "Get Apolo."

Sienna nodded and scrambled toward the door. She hated to leave, but she knew that they needed backup or none of them may get out of there alive. She was the least-experienced fighter there, so it made sense she should be the gopher. Something grabbed her leg. She snapped her head around to see Laze, though groggy, with a firm grip on her.

"No, you don't," he muttered, spitting out blood.

She swung out with her free leg, and the heel of her boot connected squarely with his jaw. His head snapped back, but he didn't let go. She kicked again and knocked him loose. Jumping to her feet, she dove toward the entrance, only to be tackled into the wall by Laze. Her head crashed into the brick wall and white spears shot through her vision. Momentarily dazed, she swung out an instant too late. Laze swiped his hand over the screen on the wall near the steel door, and her escape route slammed shut.

She elbowed him where his shirt was soaked with blood, and he was on his back a second later. He tried to get up but was knocked back when Nalea stepped on a wing. He cried out and slapped at Nalea's leg, but a second Sephian grabbed the downed Draeken's hands, banded them, and then did the same to his ankles. He gasped for air when she removed her boot from his wing.

It was then that Sienna remembered her training. Draeken wings were the most sensitive part on their bodies. She mentally kicked herself for fighting him like he was a human, and for not focusing on his weakness.

A hand grabbed her neck, and she fell back against Legian.

"Stay down," Legian growled.

She looked into feral eyes and knew there was no reasoning with him. "I need a gun."

He reached inside his coat and pulled out a small blaster. It was Legian's least favorite of all the Sephian weapons, which mean he'd carried it for her. With a smile she grabbed it, checked it, and slid it in the waistband of her skirt then turned and shoved over a stack of boxes. They didn't offer any shielding, but at least they wouldn't be sitting ducks.

"I don't suppose you brought any charges with you?" she asked above the sounds of battle.

Legian shook his head. "Blood-charges, but they won't do us any good in these close quarters."

She pulled the gun out of her belt and fired random shots through the door in the wall. She could see no Draeken, but she had no problem seeing their weapons when they stuck them around the doorway to fire. They had to be out of chaos-charges or else she would have been drowning in light and noise.

There was no way to tell if they outnumbered the Draeken or not. They were stuck in a Catch-22. They were pinned down, but at least the Draeken were faring no better. It was obvious Apolo's intel had been good.

Sienna looked around them. Definitely time for Plan B... if only she had a Plan B.

No sooner had she thought it than an earthquake shook the floor. Pieces of concrete and plaster rained down on her, even as she covered Legian with her body. Wiping dust from her eyes, she peered over the box of broken liquor bottles and saw a gaping hole where the steel door had been.

Soldiers—far more than just Bravo Team—poured into the room, hitting the deck when the Draeken started firing in their direction. "Yes!" Sienna shouted as they spanned out, many behind boxes, others running under cover fire toward the wall with the secret door.

The sound of gunfire amped up by the power of ten when machine guns went off around her. Bullets hit the brick wall outside the door, but no shots were very close. It was like the Americans were trying to miss. Her brow furrowed. Why wouldn't they want to take out the Draeken shooters?

Her eye caught an object flying through the air and through the door. Smoke hissed out through the small doorway, and the Americans stopped firing. She followed suit and watched the doorway. There were fewer shots coming through the door than before. A wing brushed through the gray haze, and she saw a Draeken turn and run, his buddy providing cover fire.

"They're getting away!"

The soldiers were moving toward the door in a synchronized manner, but they were still too far away. Sienna was closest. She jumped over the boxes. When she landed, she hit a wet patch of spilled liquor and fell. The momentum of her jump propelled her right through the door. Her foot hit the Draeken in the shin, and he went down.

No longer under fire, everyone else sprinted forward, and Legian was on the fallen Draeken at the same time a blade went for her throat. She clutched the Draeken's hand with both hers. When he was yanked back, she was able to pry the blade from his grip.

Legian yanked her to her feet. "When we get out of this—"

"I know. You'll show me how much you love me," she winked then winced, reaching for her leg. She slowly bent her knee, only to find a loose binding. With a grimace, she shoved the broken strap into the rest of the brace, checked her weapon, and motioned down the hallway, which was becoming visible through the dissipating smoke.

"I saw more Draeken head this way," she called out to the approaching soldiers.

"How many?" one of them asked.

Sienna held up a couple fingers. "At least two. Maybe three."

He nodded and yelled a command to those behind him. Then several troops stepped past them and followed him.

The group disappeared around a corner. When shots sounded, she moved forward, only to be held back by Legian.

"They've got it covered."

Sienna swallowed, trying to tamp down her adrenaline rush. She turned her attention back to the Draeken she'd drop-kicked, who was being shackled and injected with something courtesy of the Americans. It took a second before his struggles ceased and he was out cold.

The two soldiers at the downed Draeken made way for Major Sommers. He knelt by the Draeken.

Tucking the gun back into her skirt, Sienna brushed hair from her plaster dust-coated face and looked around. The place looked like Armageddon and stank like the devil had drunk himself into a stupor. "One hell of a happy hour at this place," she said to no one in particular.

She turned to Legian. "We better clear out this place before the cops show. It'll be hard to explain all this."

"There won't be any police," Major Sommers replied. "I've got that covered; it'll be harder to reign in the press. And by now, they will have received some tips. We don't need pictures of aliens circulating the papers."

Sienna shrugged. "Aliens are a daily occurrence in the tabloids."

"Yeah, but *real* pictures would be harder to explain," Jax cut in.

"Bag 'em," the major called out, causing Sienna to jerk around in time to see Nalea walking toward them, the men behind her dragging three more Draeken behind them.

"No blood?" she asked.

"Tranq guns," Jax replied. "Cleaner and safer."

"And smarter; now you have prisoners," she chimed in.

Sommers gave her a half-grin that disappeared as quickly as it had appeared. "Let's get out of here. Cleanup crew is on the way." He turned and strode away.

Sienna fell in behind him as he stepped over broken bottles and pieces of wall. Her jaw dropped as she looked around. Only one Sephian had been shot, and he was being bandaged by a curious human medic. With all that shooting, she'd expected to see a whole lot more blood. Not a single casualty. It was like an old *A-Team* episode. A thousand shots fired without any blood.

She limped behind Jax as he and the major stepped through the giant hole in the wall where the door had been minutes earlier. Steel shards jabbed out, snagging her skirt. Without pausing his stride, Legian bent down, tore the skirt, and helped her through the wall.

She looked around the vacant club. "Wow. I can't believe it's empty."

"Called in a tip of a drug bust. Cleared out the place in minutes."

She admired his ingenuity.

Sommers continued walking through the bar, and she hobbled faster to keep up. "Major?"

He slowed and glanced her way.

"Back there, the Sephians and our people worked well together, didn't they?"

"Not bad." Sommers looked from Legian to Jax and back to her. He narrowed his eyes briefly before giving a small smile. "It's a start."

Chapter Eighteen

Sienna stopped outside the door and leaned on the wall to steady herself. The new brace worked wonders, but her leg would never return to normal. Even after Doc refitted the brace after Club Mayhem—talk about a name that was so apropos—her best speed was no better than a half fast jog.

"Are you well?"

She stepped back so she could face Legian. "I'm fine." Turning around before he could reply, she punched in the code to open the door. She pushed the *drades* up her nose, and they stepped inside to the darkened room beyond.

They were early for the trinity meeting so as to give Apolo a full debrief on what had gone down with the major. She entered the lounge with Legian at her back.

Apolo stood alone, leaning with his hands on the table. He was talking to a beautiful Sephian woman on the screen. Upon Sienna and Legian's entry, he jerked around. The emotion in his eyes nearly knocked her back.

"Sorry for the disruption. We'll wait outside." She snapped around to walk away, rubbing her palms together even though the temperature in the room was almost balmy.

"Bah. Come in." He waved them in and returned his attention to the screen.

Even Legian looked timid as he stepped gingerly into the room. Sienna could make out little of the conversation, and she could tell Legian was trying to not listen while he casually inspected everything in the room except the screen. Whatever they were discussing was obviously private, and she sensed a deep longing in the words.

Krysea.

Apolo's *tahren*. The bond between the two was obvious. Every day must be torture for them. That kind of dedication to their people went far beyond anything she could imagine.

Sienna couldn't help but stare at the screen. Krysea was gorgeous. She'd expected a battle-worn, scarred woman. The Sephian leader surely couldn't be this beautiful.

Legian bumped her, nearly knocking her *drades* off. She scowled at him and his eyes looked forward. She followed his eyes and found Apolo watching her.

"Krysea wishes to speak to you." Apolo spoke with no hint of emotion.

Sienna gulped as she and Legian stepped closer to the screen and faced the leader of the Sephian people.

Legian spoke first, bowing his head and greeting the leader in Sephian. Sienna followed suit. Since her Sephian sucked, she then remained silent.

"I have begun to learn your language but have much to learn. My *tahren* will translate," Krysea said in drawn out, stilted English. Then she continued in flowing, beautiful Sephian.

Apolo translated. "Krysea blesses your bond and prays for a blissful future."

"Thank you," Sienna said. Legian echoed her.

Krysea nodded with a warm smile before continuing.

"She has been apprised of your actions and approves my choice," Apolo added, his voice and manner all-business.

Sienna glanced over at him. "Choice?"

Apolo narrowed his eyes onto her. "Regarding you."

He said something else but she missed it, and jerked her attention back to the screen. Krysea was still speaking. The leader smiled, and the screen when black.

Apolo stared at the blank screen. The tightness in his body betrayed his emotionless face.

"How do you do it? Stay apart from Krysea, I mean," Sienna asked softly in his direction.

He jerked out of his trance and looked up to face her. "I do it because I must."

Apolo let out a deep breath. To her, it sounded like hopelessness. He looked up, and she could have sworn his eyes were damp.

"It took us several months at full power to fly here; we nearly used up our long-range power cells. That was intentional. The cells are rechargeable, and initial planetary analysis showed that your star generated energy similar to ours, which can recharge our power cells. Unfortunately, when we arrived, we learned that was not the case. Your sun does not generate compatible energy. Even if we tried to return on our lowest power settings, we'd never make it. We are running our base off our short-range power cells now, but they won't last a year. At that point we will be fully dependent on this planet's resources."

Sienna brought a hand over her mouth. "You're stranded here?"

Apolo shook his head. "We are looking for other options, but haven't found anything viable. The only good news is that the Draeken run off the same energy source and likely discovered the same problem when they arrived here."

"Earth is our home now." Legian spoke quietly, his voice barely a whisper.

"Can't Krysea send more ships with large power cells?"

Legian shook his head. "The cells are too large to transport. They can't send enough to bring us all back, and any ship sent here would be stranded as well."

"I'm so sorry." Sienna's voice cracked as her heart broke. She and Apolo may not see eye to eye all the time, but no *tahren* should be separated. To be separated like that was an unending torture. A death sentence.

Apolo cracked his neck and walked around the table. "Take a seat until the rest of the trinity and Jax arrive."

She glanced up at Legian, who nodded to her. "Apolo, we would like to debrief you about what happened at Mayhem."

Apolo waved her off. "Excellent progress with the humans; the debrief can wait until after the meeting." He started to pace.

Frowning, Sienna sat in the nearest chair. Legian sat down next to her, and together they endured the ominous silence. It took five interminable minutes before the others arrived, and during that time she watched a frazzled Apolo transition back into the stoic leader she'd come to respect.

First to the room were Bente and Jax, who'd become friends over past few weeks. Nalea finally arrived, a few minutes late. Ever since the base attack, she seemed distracted, unfocused. Something was up, but her friend's style was to keep things bottled up, festering, until they exploded like a Molotov cocktail. Sienna made a mental note to schedule some time with her. Legian had told her once about the last time Nalea had lost it. It wasn't pretty. Evidently, people died when Nalea blew.

Sienna didn't know exactly what had happened the previous time; Legian said it had had something to do with Nalea's family. Nalea never spoke of her family. In fact, no one knew anything about her childhood. That was, until a guy showed up who swore he'd worked under the same Draeken house as Nalea, and that he knew her secret. No one had thought anything of it until the next day when Nalea and the guy went missing, along with a ship. She'd shown back up a week later. Alone, nearly starved, and without a ship. She had claimed they'd gone on a recon flight and were shot down, but no one knew the truth, other than the fact that no recon flight had been scheduled. Legian suspected it was intentional that she came back alone, but he'd never dared confront her on it.

Nalea nodded to Sienna on her way around the table to her chair.

Apolo started before everyone sat down. "The Mayhem mission dealt a small blow to the Draeken. From what I've heard, we can thank Jax for the human assistance at the club. Without them, we very likely would have suffered losses. As it stands, we were very fortunate to incur no casualties, with only one of us acquiring minor wounds."

Applause lightened the atmosphere.

Apolo continued. "The mission reopened the door for discussions. I have spoken with Colonel Jerrick and have arranged for an official alliance meeting that will include him as well as a political leader. The meeting should be at a location that has connections to both our people. Therefore, I have requested Sienna's cabin."

Sienna jerked upright. "My cabin? Are you sure?"

Apolo smiled. He had *that* look again. The one he always had before he dropped a bomb.

"What?" she asked, the word barely a whisper.

"Since you became Legian's *tahren*, you have been thrown through a quantum hole. Most would have broken. Many would not have survived. Yet, your prowess at both defending the base during the attack and on the Mayhem mission has earned the respect of the Sephians based here on this planet, of me, and most importantly, of our *tahcayaren*, Krysea. You and I often have different views, and it is those differences that I have come to value the most. Earth is our new home. It is time we acclimate to our new world and, hopefully, new people."

Apolo looked at each member of his trinity in turn. "I will always do what is best for my people. And, it is in their best interest that I made my decision. From this point forward, Sienna shall become the human face for the Sephians on Earth."

Sienna frowned. "I don't understand."

"Sephians are a matriarchal society. It is time to bring a human female to the helm of this base. It brings strength to our troops. While Jax advises me from a military perspective, I will look to you, Sienna, to advise me on how best to integrate our peoples."

"I don't know what to say." And she didn't. Of all the words out of Apolo's mouth, what she'd just heard was far from what she'd expected. While her logical mind knew it was purely a political ploy to set the stage for human-Sephian relations, her emotional heart remained in shock.

"Do you accept this responsibility?" Apolo asked.

She looked around the room. Every eye was on her. She had always been a loner. An introvert. This kind of responsibility should belong to someone who was bred for it, not some country girl who played Xbox. But she also didn't believe in coincidences; Legian crashing in her backyard had been the first step, leading to where she now stood.

She squeezed Legian's hand before looking back to Apolo. "I graciously accept this honor."

Apolo walked over and held out his arm, and they sealed the pact Sephian-style—by clasping each other's forearms.

"According to Sephian tradition, I have a trinity, a body of three minds to guide me and with whom I can discuss all topics of importance." Apolo turned to Legian, Bente, and Nalea before turning back to Sienna. "While you can consult with me any time, I hope you will also look to my trinity to guide you."

Sienna made eye contact with each of the trinity members. "Of course. I look forward to your guidance, friendship, and honest thoughts." She turned to Jax. "I'll look to Jax as well." She smiled. "You haven't let me down yet."

Apolo nodded. "I believe their counsel will guide you well." His voice held a hint of respect. "Now, let's make the announcement and break out the drinks."

She strode over to Legian and he embraced her. Even if it was purely for show, one thing was for sure: she wouldn't let them down. She'd make a good poster child for relations. She would see it through to the end. No matter what.

Chapter Nineteen

Sienna had never been more stressed in her life. More
than when she discovered aliens weren't some made-up
sci-fi creatures from Mars. More than when she left the life
she knew behind and went traipsing off into the unknown
with one of those aliens. More than when the base was
attacked and she'd nearly been killed. More than any of that.

She now knew what Atlas must have felt like to bear the
weight of the world on his shoulders. Of course, her responsibility didn't come near that. She was just a figurehead
rather than an actual decision-maker. Still, she was the
walking commercial for integrating Sephians into the world.
After all, she was the first human to have a *tahren*.

She wished she could fade into the SUV's black leather so
she wouldn't have to go back to her cabin. They were already
driving down familiar rough side roads. It wouldn't be much
longer now.

The truth was she'd never had to be responsible for
anyone else but herself before. Even with Bobby. He had been
away on duty too often and at home too little. It had left her
to remain carefree and—she hated to admit it—selfish. But

suddenly, for the first time in her life, how she acted could impact others' lives.

Her greatest fear wasn't looking bad in front of others; that she could live with. Her greatest fear also wasn't Apolo realizing he had made a mistake. Or of those closest to her seeing that she couldn't hack it. Or even those who had seen and done shit she'd only imagined who would see through her in a heartbeat if she faltered and would know that she had been faking it all along, that she didn't have the guts to make the tough calls.

No, her greatest fear was that her actions could lead to death. That was something she wasn't sure she could handle.

Legian squeezed her hand. "Is everything okay?"

She put on a fake smile. "First day on the job jitters, that's all."

He kissed the top of her head. "You'll do fine. Apolo will be there. You won't be alone. You will never be alone."

"Yeah." Sienna grinned, and then stared out the window at the passing trees. It was true. She knew she wasn't alone. With them, she would never feel alone.

Sienna leaned forward and squeezed Jax's shoulder. "Thanks for driving."

"No problem. I'm a piss-poor backseat driver. I'll take driving any day over being a passenger."

"What do we need to do before your father arrives?" Risa asked Jax from beside him in the front seat.

"We'll need to set up a perimeter in case the news leaked to the Draeken," Legian answered.

Jax answered. "Ace checked out the place a couple of days ago, so we should be all set. The cabin and surrounding woods will be secure."

"He's your army buddy, right?" Risa asked.

Jax nodded.

"So, Lea," Sienna said. "If I remember right, we're due for

a girls' night involving some wine you've been hiding in your room."

Nalea smiled in response, snapping her attention back inside the vehicle. "The wine's still there, safe and sound."

"We're here," Jax called out from the front, his voice turning soldier-serious in a split second.

Conversation over, she looked out the window. Her heart gave a little jump. Home. Only it wasn't home. Not anymore. Sienna had never thought she'd see the place again. It looked exactly as she'd left it. The small stone cabin stood in a scant clearing within dense pine woods. She'd built it for the privacy and had always found solace there, surrounded by sounds of bird songs and pine needles rustling in the breeze.

She couldn't even begin to fathom how homesick the Sephians must be, knowing they never would see their home again. She stepped out of the SUV and inhaled the forest air. It was cool and laden with the woodsy scent of evergreen. Spring was beginning to show its blooms, though winter was still hanging on for all it was worth. She walked around the matching SUVs already parked nearby and took in the building before her. *Home.*

The colonel and others weren't scheduled to arrive until twilight when the Sephians could cope without dark glasses. She'd wanted to come early to have some time at her cabin. But as she stepped through the door, a bustle of activity filled the small space. Her home had become claustrophobic, and she bit back the tension. There hadn't been this many people here even when the construction crew had built the place.

With her mother off touring the world, she'd never found the time to see the house her daughter built. Not that Sienna hadn't expected that. Kat had always made it clear that work was more important. Sienna loved her mother—that never in question—but her mother wasn't the warm and fuzzy type. She believed good parenting involved exposing children to the ugliness in the world by the time they could walk.

Once Sienna hit eighteen, her parents had shipped her off to college. She'd wanted to stay with them and join their humanitarian crew, but they'd had different ideas. They seemed to think college was a necessity. Considering her an adult, they put Sienna on the first flight back to the States.

She may not have had a loving childhood, but for the first time in her life she was thankful for her parents. They had taught her life was tough. They had also fervently believed that there was life beyond the stars. What would have happened to Legian if he'd crashed in a skeptic's backyard? And she'd learned one critical thing while raising herself out of a suitcase: no matter what happened, she could deal with it. It was a lesson she'd used over and over again with the Sephians.

She sensed Legian come up behind her before he touched her. "You are my rock," she murmured as he wrapped his arms around her.

"I don't understand the statement. I don't consider myself like a stone, although parts of me become hard as one."

She twirled in his arms to find a grin on his face.

"Let's go for a walk." He gruffly took her hand and led her outdoors.

Nearly an hour later, they sauntered back into the cabin.

Nalea winked at her. "You still have a branch in your hair."

"Nice to see you two could make it," Jax said, walking from the kitchen eating a real, honest-to-goodness cheeseburger.

Her stomach growled, and she grabbed the half-eaten burger from his hand.

"I was eating that."

She took a big bite of the juicy burger. "Perks of being a model citizen," she said with a very full mouth.

He shrugged, walked back into the kitchen and returned seconds later with another one. "The security perimeter has been set up. We have full video. Had it three hours now."

She stopped chewing. "How far out does the perimeter go?"

He smirked. "Far enough to see which tree you carved your names into."

———

Another hour later—because Legian definitely did not behave in the shower—Sienna reached for the doorknob, poised for the meeting. She paused, turned, and looked around.

Nothing had changed. Everything looked exactly as she'd left it. Surprising, since Jax's team—and possibly the police— had rifled through every square inch of the cabin. Sienna moved to the dresser, opened the small wood box on the top of it, and pulled out the silver charm bracelet. A charm for every trip she and Bobby had taken, a charm for every special occasion. At least, that had been the plan. Only a couple of the links had charms. Their time had been cut far too short. When he died, she'd thought she had, too. Maybe that was the real reason why she'd built a cabin so far out in the woods. To avoid connecting with anyone else.

And then life went on. She'd found out she hadn't died with Bobby. Instead, she had plenty of life left. It had just been buried under grit and grime.

"Ready for this?" Legian asked as he came up behind her.

She placed the bracelet back in the box, closed it, and stepped toward the door. She smoothed her hands down her loose linen sweater and khaki cargos before reaching for the doorknob again. "I am ready." She took a deep breath, opened the door, and stepped into the hallway beyond.

A fire was lit in the living room, giving the area a comfortable, homey feel. Apolo had been right. Her home was a perfect location for this meeting. You couldn't get more human than a cabin.

"Hey, Sienna."

She turned to see Nalea standing nearby. "Sorry. I didn't see you."

"The humans will be here any minute, but there's still no sign of Apolo. Have you heard from him?"

Sienna grabbed her phone, even though Apolo had never called her on it before. No missed calls. "No one's heard from him?"

"I'm afraid not. He's usually early to all functions."

At that moment, Apolo's SUV pulled into the drive and Sienna rushed out to meet them.

The back door of the SUV swung open and she grabbed it. Apolo looked pissed off, but otherwise unharmed. "Where have you been?"

Apolo motioned toward the front of the vehicle. "Bente got us lost."

"Fucking address isn't on the nav system," Bente spewed out as he stalked past her.

She smiled and caught up with Bente. "You could fly light years through space and find a little planet in the middle of the universe, but you couldn't find a cabin in the woods less than fifty miles from the base?"

"Piss off," was the Sephian's reply, and he opened the screen door, letting it snap back shut in front of her. Bente wasn't exactly a gentleman. He could make bad guys in the movies look warm and cuddly. Then again, she guessed warm and cuddly would've been pretty useless during a war. No wonder he was so popular with Sephian women. If he wasn't there to kill you, a girl could feel pretty safe with him around.

She caught the door into the cabin before it smacked her in the face.

"What the hell kind of food is this?" Bente grumbled from the kitchen, and she walked toward his voice.

He was holding a cheeseburger in one hand, examining it like it had wiggled.

"It's called food. And trust me, our guests are going to like these a whole lot better than the crap you like so much," she said with a visible shudder.

Nalea looked up from her chair by the window and came to her feet. "You made it."

Apolo grimaced. "Yes, just some minor delays. Any word from our guests?"

"Ace says they're less than a mile out," Jax replied. Jax lifted his hand. "Wait. No. They're driving in now." He stepped outside without another word.

"Game on." She stood and followed Apolo outside.

Several black Humvees pulled up in a semi-circle around the front of the cabin and soldiers poured out. She recognized Colonel Jerrick and Major Sommers right away. A couple of suits walked with them, each protected on all sides by soldiers in two different types of uniforms. American and British.

Jax stepped up first and saluted his father. The older Jerrick returned it with a haphazard salute before continuing toward the house. He stopped a few feet away.

Sienna nodded to each in turn. "Good to see you again, Colonel. Major. Welcome to my home."

The colonel held out his hand, which she accepted. "Thank you for hosting us, Ms. Wolfe." He turned to Apolo. "Apolo. I can only hope that tonight's meeting is less exciting and far more productive."

"As do I, Colonel. The perimeter has been secured by both your and my people. I believe you will find security up to your standards."

The officer nodded then motioned to the men standing at his side. "I'd like to introduce Senator Dane Sokolos of the U.S. Senate and Lieutenant-Colonel Geoffrey Bryant of the British Army."

After a flurry of introductions, Sienna opened the door. "Shall we go inside where it is more comfortable, gentlemen?"

The group filled the living room. Apolo stood to her left with Jax and Bente on his other side. Legian and Nalea stepped in on her right.

"The Draeken showed first aggression at the club," the colonel said as he sat down on the sofa. Evidently not one to mince words, he got right down to business. "As such, we believe is it in the best interest of our countries to treat the Draeken as a likely threat. We also believe that an arrangement would be beneficial between our people and yours."

Apolo smiled with a slight nod. "That is what we desire. By combining forces, we can eradicate the Draeken threat."

Jerrick lifted a finger. "Our stance is not to eradicate an entire race. Rather, we want to gather more information and perhaps engage the Draeken, while insulating our people against harm."

"Ideally," Lieutenant-Colonel Bryant interjected in a smooth British accent. "While the United Kingdom has no desire in becoming embroiled in a costly war, we will not stand idly by if the Draeken attack our allies and attempt to build an empire across the ocean."

Apolo spoke slowly and warmly. "Then our goals are common. I believe a partnership can be devised to secure our common interests."

Jerrick leaned forward. "And I'm most curious about what

some of those interests may be, Apolo."

Apolo gave a slight tilt of his head. "I see you appreciate candor, Colonel, so I'll lay it out. We exhausted our power supplies when we followed the Draeken to your world. We cannot return to Sephia. We offer our knowledge and technology in return for amnesty, full citizenship, and your support to reveal ourselves to the world's leaders."

Jerrick rubbed his chin while the room sat in silence, considering Apolo's words. The senator, who Sienna recognized as being from Arkansas, spoke first. "An agreement like that would need to be formalized first by the American President, and then the United Nations Security Council would need to accept it. Following that, it must be communicated to the public in the right way and at the right time. It won't be easy introducing your people to the general population. We can expect riots, both from the human rights and the religious fronts, as well as the racists. And that's just for starters."

Sienna swallowed before speaking. "It will change the way we've always looked at ourselves. We're no longer alone in the universe, and we have to learn to accept that there are other races as intelligent as us. It wasn't easy for me, and I imagine it was no easier for you. It will be the biggest change ever to be announced to the world. However, as leaders, you have the power to embrace the opportunity and announce us to the world in your own way and at a time of your choosing, or else have the Draeken do it for you. You can usher in a new age of enlightenment."

"Sienna speaks the truth," Apolo added. "We are not forcing your decision. The decision is yours. We will maintain a covert base as long as the Draeken threat permits, knowing we remain under your goodwill. However, the Draeken have made no such promises. And from what we saw at the club, the Draeken will quickly become much more than urban legends. What have you learned from the Draeken prisoners you attained at the club?"

"Unfortunately, very little," Sommers replied. "We had no proof of their existence until last week. We have begun to study the Draeken we captured. They haven't spoken yet, but biologically speaking, they have been a goldmine of information so far."

Sienna cringed inwardly at the implication of his words. Visions of mice in cages surrounded by white lab coats came to mind. No one, not even the Draeken, deserved to be lab experiments.

She picked up a small briefcase. "Within weeks of landing on our world, Sephian computer systems designed a vaccine for the common cold. Sephian knowledge and technology are generations ahead of ours, and they are willing to share all that in exchange for an alliance. This case contains several vials of the vaccine, and memory sticks with the formula and all the medical data you need to prove that it works with no negative side effects. I have taken it and suffered no ill effect. Consider this token as a gift to show the depth of Sephian intent and goodwill." She opened the case and walked around to show it to the men in the room.

Jerrick accepted the case, snapped it shut, and handed it to the soldier at his right. "I believe our intentions are aligned. I have the authority to formalize a temporary arrangement with the Sephians from a military perspective. We will work together to mitigate the Draeken threat, under certain conditions, of course."

"Of course," Apolo said and shook the colonel's hand.

It was the senator's turn next. "While we cannot commit to a formal agreement today, I give you my word that the proposal will be brought to the President. Your act of good faith will go far in earning our trust. I'll be in touch to discuss an arrangement in more detail."

Senator Sokolos held out his hand, and again Apolo accepted.

"Lieutenant-Colonel Bryant," Apolo spoke, and the British officer turned his attention to the Sephian leader. "I have a proposal for you."

"Go ahead," Bryant replied.

"Having the entire Sephian force in one location is a risk that has plagued me since we came to your world. A risk that became a reality when the Draeken attacked our base. I propose we will split the Sephian force, with half staying in North America, and half relocating to the UK. You would select the location, of course. You may also station key personnel at the location to learn from us. It would provide an opportunity for us to work alongside one another while better protecting the Sephian people and our knowledge of the Draeken. What say you to this?"

Bryant sat quiet for a moment, and then came to his feet abruptly. "Since there's plenty of hand shaking going on today, why not some more." He smiled. "I came here to propose the same. In fact, I already have a location being prepared. As such, I accept your proposal, and I believe we will learn much from one another."

The two men shook hands.

One of the soldiers stepped forward holding something in his hand. Sienna jumped at the movement.

The senator gestured to the soldier. "We'd like some photographs of this momentous occasion. This meeting will be considered First Contact in the history books."

"Of course," Apolo said.

The men came to stand near Apolo. The trinity, Jax, and Sienna stood behind Apolo. Sienna stood with a practiced smile, oblivious to the flashes of the camera. She had bigger things on her mind. Alliances were being formed, but what if they failed?

Chapter Twenty

S ienna's day began with an envelope. A small, discreet manila envelope slid under her bedroom door.

She lifted Legian's arm and slid out from under him and climbed out of bed, the old wrought iron bed creaking as she did so. A large hand reached out and wrapped around her waist, pulling her back toward him.

"Come back to bed," he mumbled dreamily.

She twirled out of his arm and he grumbled. Ignoring him, she pulled on the old terry cloth robe she'd had for twenty years. It had been hanging on the hook by the bed, exactly where she'd left it on the night she joined the Sephians.

Not ready to spend ten minutes putting her brace on, she reached for the walking stick that was propped in the corner. Using it for support, she limped over to the door and picked up the envelope and turned it over. It was sealed shut. An intricate design decorated the front. No writing.

Legian pulled himself up to an elbow. "What is it?"

"Don't know. The envelope only has a symbol on it. Do you recognize it?" She held it up, and his face visibly paled.

In a burst, he jumped out of bed, grabbed her wrist, and pulled the envelope from her hand. He became hard as a statue.

"I take it you recognize the symbol?"

Legian grimaced. She could feel his fear down to her toes.

She pulled back and looked into his eyes. "What is it?"

"It's the imperial symbol of the Draeken."

She suddenly had a hard time swallowing. "How'd it get here? We have twenty-four-hour security and surveillance on the cabin. There's no way in hell a Draeken got in here."

"Nevertheless, you are holding a letter with the Draeken imperial symbol on it." He rushed to put on his clothes. "I will go over the video from the past several hours. If we have a traitor here, I will find him."

She nodded mutely before looking from the envelope to him and back again. "We've got to open it."

Legian nodded tightly.

She gently tugged the envelope from his grip then tore off the end and held the open end down. A small piece of paper slid out onto her palm.

"What's it say?" he asked while she examined both sides of the paper.

"It says *Cave. Noon. Today.*"

Legian frowned. "Do you have any idea where this cave is?"

Neither spoke for what seemed like eternity. Finally, she broke the silence. "I'm thinking we should go to see what's up."

"It's a trap."

"If they wanted to ambush us, why not do it at the cabin while we slept? If they could slide an envelope under my door without being noticed, they could just as easily assassinate us in our sleep. Besides, if it were a trap, why would they be so obvious about it? Invite us to a trap? That's so cliché."

Legian started to pace. Like Apolo, he did that whenever he thought. She swore he'd worn a path into the floor in their room back at the base. He stopped before she expected him to. "We'll set troops up around the area. I'll go in at noon to draw them out."

She put her hands on her hips and glared. "No. This letter has to be meant for both of us. You recognized the Draeken seal, and I'm the only one who'd know about the cave."

"We can't risk it."

She drew in a deep breath and let it out slowly. She didn't want to do it, but she had to. "Would you say the same to anyone else?"

His lack of response was answer enough.

"Fine," she continued. "You're my *tahren*. I want and respect your advice. But it's my life and my decision. The letter is meant for us. I'm going."

"That is not practical," Legian gritted out through clenched teeth.

"It's safe to say they know about last night's meeting if they know we're here. What if they're ready to surrender or make some kind of peace offering?"

"You don't know the Draeken like I do."

"I know. That's why I trust your guidance. But you're not being objective. You want me to stay back for my protection, not for the good of our people."

"That's not true."

"It's true," she snapped. "If this is something that can shorten this war, I want to be there. End of discussion. The video should show us who delivered it. We can ask more questions then. In the meantime, I trust you and Jax to make sure the perimeter is safe so we're not walking into a trap."

He glared at her for a moment. "As you wish," he

muttered before handing the note back to her and stomping off to the bathroom.

She stared at the closed bathroom door for a moment. She knew Legian only had her safety in mind, but she couldn't be respected if she let him coddle her.

She didn't bother with getting dressed. She stepped out into the hall and hobbled through to the living room. Jax and Risa were already sitting on the couch, eating egg sandwiches. Nalea sat across from them, eying their food with suspicion.

Risa took a bite out of her sandwich.

Nalea cringed. "How can you eat the egg of an animal? That is so wrong."

"Easy," Risa replied. "Like this." And at that moment, both she and Jax took oversized bites out of their sandwiches.

Now Nalea shuddered. "This planet has barbaric practices."

"Barbaric, but tasty," Sienna replied.

"Let me make you one." Risa jumped up, licking butter from her fingers. "I'm really getting into this cooking thing."

"And she's pretty good at it," Jax added, leaning back contentedly on the couch.

"Yeah, I'll take one. Thanks." Sienna collapsed into a seat. "Hey, have either of you seen anything odd around here this morning?"

"No, why?" Nalea asked.

Sienna handed over the letter and envelope to Nalea.

Her face paled, as Legian's had done minutes earlier. "Where did you get this?"

"Someone slid it under my bedroom door. Legian is going to check out the videos."

Jax popped to his feet, walked over, and grabbed the letter.

"It's from the Draeken."

He frowned and grabbed his radio. "Ace, check in."

"Ace, here."

"Alert the teams. I need a full perimeter check. We have a breach. Possible Draeken," Jax said into the radio.

"Copy that," Ace replied.

Jax turned back to face Sienna. "Are you going?"

She nodded. "Can you and Legian make sure we're ready for whatever they try?"

"Of course," Jax replied. "I need you to show me the area on a map. I'll have the area secure within the hour. We'll have eyes on the ground. And, I'll be with you at the meeting."

"I'm coming, too," Nalea replied, matter-of-factly.

Sienna smiled. "Thank you. I can't ask any of you to come. Like Legian said, it could be a trap, but—"

"We stand together," Legian interrupted as he approached.

Relief washed over Sienna when Nalea and Jax nodded their agreement, and she returned a smile. "Thanks, guys."

"What'd I miss?"

Sienna glanced up to see Risa walking into the room, carrying a plate with a steaming egg sandwich on it. The med-tech gasped and dropped the plate. Glass shattered across the stone floor. She pointed to the envelope as she knelt and began to pick up the glass shards. "What's that?"

"It seems Sienna has received an invitation to a party," Nalea replied.

Jax knelt and helped Risa collect pieces on the floor.

Nalea ran a hand through her hair. "But it doesn't make sense. How did the letter get into this cabin in the first place? We have a full perimeter line set up."

"My guess?" Sienna replied. "It came from the inside."

"You mean the traitor's here? With us? I thought we were

safe." Risa started to shake. Jax rubbed her back while whispering soothing words in her ear.

Sienna paid no attention to Risa, and instead focused on calming her own nerves. The one thing she didn't need today was more stress. Jax could deal with his woman. "It's a half-hour ride out to the cave on ATVs. We have a lot to do and only five hours to do it in. Let's get busy." She turned around and headed down the hall. She had plenty to do, starting with a long, hot shower to get some thinking done.

Sienna strapped on a helmet and climbed onto her ATV. Legian climbed on behind her while Nalea rode with Jax on one of the new ATVs they'd brought when setting up security around the cabin. Even though it was a cloudy day, both Sephians wore dark sunglasses to protect their eyes.

Nalea and Jax both wore earpieces and spoke with the Sephians and soldiers posted around the perimeter. The entire makeshift base was on full alert, and guards were positioned throughout the woods around the cave. The air buzzed with energy. Unfortunately, they were going in none the wiser than when she'd found the letter in the morning. The cameras had conspicuously cut out for an entire hour before sunrise, leaving them with a big fat zilch for leads. They weren't even one step closer to knowing who—or what—had delivered that letter.

With a swift movement of her foot, the ATV jumped into gear, and they began the ride deeper into the woods.

They all wore black Sephian uniforms. Not for a fashion statement, but because they were durable and did a great job of keeping off sharp tree branches and tiny critters, both of which infested these woods. The thin fabric also worked better than anything with her leg brace. Any of her other pants jammed up in the bands.

The weather was perfect, and it took under twenty minutes to get to the cave. Still concealed by brush, they had to get within ten feet of the entrance to see it. Legian jumped off the quad before she stopped, and began looking for signs of others in the area. Jax and Nalea were right behind him. Sienna moved more gingerly, taking in anything that may have changed since the last time she was here.

She didn't have to wait long. Tattooed wings spread out as a Draeken she recognized emerged from the cave entrance. She stood firm. Her friends swiftly came to her, setting up a living, breathing wall of protection.

"Hello, Roden." Sienna was as polite as possible, while a phantom pain in her leg was busy reminding her of why she disliked that particular Draeken so much.

"Sienna Wolfe." He continued walking toward her, a Draeken woman and a Draeken man flanking his sides. He hadn't changed a bit. His silver hair was still long, and he looked like he could knock out Wolverine in a single punch. His wing even looked like it had healed completely. Not even the tattoos were marred. She wished she'd been so lucky. He wore a dark kilt, boots, and a tight shirt—all with pockets and weapons strapped to them.

Sienna scanned his bodyguards. Both were dressed similarly to Roden. Easily six feet tall, the woman reminded her of a Valkyrie with her long silver hair—the wings suiting her perfectly. The man on Roden's other side looked feral, his cold eyes vacant of all emotion, of all humanity. *He's already dead. Except his body's still going.*

Roden glanced over everyone with Sienna until his eyes stopped on the woman standing to her left. "Ah. *Nalea.* I was hoping you'd make an appearance. Did you come here to continue what we started?" He drawled out her name with sugary seduction. It gave Sienna a sick feeling. The bastard knew exactly how to push buttons. He was dangerous.

Nalea's nostrils flared, and she pulled out a blaster.

Sienna placed her hand on her friend's forearm, and Nalea slowly lowered her blaster a couple inches. "Ignore him," Sienna muttered under her breath.

"Easier said than done," the Draeken crooned in a deep, masculine voice.

She pointed a finger at Roden. "You. Behave. Or I'll let her shoot you. Now, are you going to tell us why we're here, or did you schedule this little meeting simply to make jabs?"

A corner of his mouth curled upward. "No wonder you aligned with the Sephians. You have the same violent streak. Have you noticed? You'll never see Draeken drawing first blood in any conflict. Regardless of the inherent violence in you and your chosen race, I have a proposition for you, dear Sienna."

Legian sidestepped and became a wall in front of her. He spoke with his fists clenched. "That is my *tahren* you speak to, Draeken. Take care with your words."

Roden snarled back. "Your *tahren* is the reason I'm here, Sephian scum."

She put a hand on Legian's shoulder and stepped forward. "You have quite the way with folks, Roden."

He took a casual step closer to her, as if she didn't have three armed bodyguards at her side. "It's simple. Death starts wars. Life ends wars. I have a proposal to end the genocide of my people."

She raised an eyebrow.

"Surely your *tahren* told you how my people have been driven to near extinction? Those few of us who remain survived only by fleeing our home."

Nalea nearly spat the words. "Sephia was never your home."

"I disagree, woman."

"The name's Nalea," Sienna said. "And you digress."

"No, Sienna. It's important that you understand our history if we are to attain peace," he replied. The woman next to him lifted her chin slightly, never once taking her eyes off Sienna.

Jax and Legian remained alongside her, but she suspected Legian was doing the best he could to not rip the heads off the Draeken right then and there. She considered letting him do it. Maybe it would end the war. Then again, it could cause an all-out war on Earth.

"I'm sure you have heard of the Great Rebellion—what the Sephians call the Noble War?" Roden asked.

"I have. It was where the Sephians reclaimed their world from their enslavers."

He narrowed his eyes slightly. "Hmm. But have you been told of how we came to Sephia in the first place?"

"No one knows the truth, Draeken," Legian spat out through clenched teeth.

Roden scowled. "No one knows, because the Sephians destroyed the records shortly after the Great War. But answer this, Sephian. Why would they destroy their own historical records unless those files showed something they didn't want their successors to remember?"

The Draeken then turned from Legian to Sienna. "You see, the star that illuminated our home world had grown old. Our people were given a choice. Flee our dying planet and possibly die in the frozen expansion of space, or stay and die at home in a guaranteed fiery death. Millions fled in large ships. Some went off on their own, but most ships stayed together and traveled through the light years."

"Get on with it. I grow tired of your stories," Legian muttered.

"I would if I didn't keep getting interrupted," the Draeken

replied dryly. "Now, where was I? Oh, yes. Eventually, our ships ran low on provisions. After all, they were massively over capacity and couldn't support the numbers on them long-term. Fortunately, our systems showed our people to a planet with no suns. It was a bleak world, far different from our bright, warm world, but it sustained life. That was what mattered. The Draeken leaders offered alms in the form of technology and knowledge to the Sephians in return for approval to form a settlement on-world. The Sephians callously rejected our offer. Then our people begged. Again, they were rejected. My people were running out of food and had months to live. Again, they were forced to make a hard choice. They chose to fight for survival."

Nalea moved but didn't leave Sienna's side. "That is just a legend. We have our own, and it doesn't paint the Draeken nearly as pretty."

He shrugged. "So you say. But, what matters is that we won the Great War, and therefore won the right to live on Sephia."

"And we won the Noble War," Legian replied, "and reclaimed our home. And we vowed you would never turn another people into your slaves again."

Roden shrugged. "Your world had slavery before we ever got there. We just continued that Sephian tradition. And who says that's what we're doing on this world?" he snapped.

"You're Draeken. That's what you do." Nalea's words sizzled with scorn. The tension was so palpable, Sienna felt herself breathing more rapidly.

"We're Draeken. We survive. *That* is what we do, Nalea." He murmured her name softly, and Sienna watched her friend prickle in response.

"Thanks for the history lesson, Roden," Sienna said. "So, why did you really come here today?"

Roden cracked his knuckles, and she noticed Jax put his

hand on his holster at the movement. The Draeken noticed it, too, because the woman next to Roden matched Jax's stance.

"I offer a quid pro quo, Sienna. You know the position I carry, and the power I wield. With a snap of my fingers, I could have you killed. Or, I could use that power to end the war."

"Likewise," Sienna snarled.

"The war is over," Legian said. "You lost. Now we're just doing cleanup."

Roden glared at Legian. "The war will never be over. Not until the two races align."

"And how do you plan to accomplish that?" Sienna asked.

"As I declared before, life ends wars."

Sienna's eyebrows lifted. "You're going to have to elaborate. Spell it out for me."

"Simple. We unite the people by uniting the leaders. You will become my mate—"

Sienna couldn't hear anything else because Legian lurched forward and grabbed Roden by the neck. Roden punched him, knocking him back. The other two Draeken stepped forward, keeping their hands on their holsters. Jax jumped in and pulled Legian back.

Roden sported a bloody nose, and Legian looked like he was going to have a heck of a shiner.

Sienna scowled. "Are you two done? Now can we talk again?" She looked straight at Roden. "You were saying?"

He grinned, and then he frowned and spat blood. "I know you have a *tahren*. On this world, you could have chosen none higher in status. Except for Apolo that is, but he is already taken and Krysea's not here, so that no longer matters. By taking me as your consort, you—the human—unite both the Sephians and the Draeken while also bringing in the human element."

She squinted. "What part of *tahren* don't you understand?"

"I take it your *tahren* failed to mention that, in both our races, women in authority can have more than one cohort. It has been done in the past to unite people. I have no doubt it would work here."

Sienna's knees grew wobbly, though she remained standing. Out of everything she had prepared for today, a marriage proposal wasn't one of them. Especially from a being who had tried to kill her.

Roden's gaze moved to Nalea. He looked up and down like he was undressing her. "However, one of Apolo's elite trinity would serve as a suitable second choice to unite our two races on this new world. The human element is merely a nice political statement."

Nalea snarled and Roden smiled. "I'm nobody's second choice," she gritted out before lunging at him.

Sienna saw a shimmer in the light and noticed the knife Nalea gripped. "Lea, no!"

The other two Draeken pulled out their blasters, and Legian and Jax did the same. Sienna expected to feel the pain of being shot. Instead, she was knocked to the ground. She looked up to see Legian roll off her and start firing at the Draeken. Shots were returned.

Dark gold liquid flowed from his shoulder. "Damn it, Legian. You got shot."

"Only a flesh wound," he muttered.

She pushed him behind the trunk of the tree. Sienna couldn't see anything. Legian blocked her view. "Stay here," she ordered, and then jumped behind the next tree. She looked around the large trunk and caught a glimpse of Jax firing his gun while running in a crouched position toward where the Draeken had been standing before she was knocked to the ground.

She fired several shots into the air in case the Sephians had lost contact with Nalea. Something caught her eye. She turned in time to be grabbed by the Draeken male.

He tackled her to the ground, and her weak leg twisted under his weight. Pain shot through her, but she pushed the pain back by clenching her teeth. Her attacker had been shot at least twice, but he moved like he was in no pain. He lifted a knife. She let out a war cry, jerked her gun to him, and squeezed the trigger point blank at his chest.

She couldn't say how many times she shot him. All she knew was that she held the trigger down until there was a hole where his chest had been. As his body fell, Legian caught it and threw it to the side. He then pulled her to her feet and looked her over for wounds. Only after he had convinced himself she was okay did he pull her to him.

Sienna clutched Legian's arms around her waist as she stared at the corpse. She'd never killed so close before. She thought she was going to be sick.

Voices jarred her from her thoughts. She turned to Legian. Her eyes widened when she remembered he was wounded and slapped her hand over his shoulder.

He winced and wrapped his hand around her wrist but didn't pull it away. "Save your strength," he murmured.

"Trust me. I've got enough energy for both of us," she replied and kept her hand in place, the warmth buzzing under her palm. With her adrenaline high, she felt like she could heal every wounded Sephian in a ten-mile radius. For seconds—or minutes—they watched each other, unafraid of each other's gaze.

Once the heat between Legian's shoulder and her hand returned to normal, she pulled away and put her hand in his. Together, they walked back toward the cave. Reinforcements had arrived and were scanning the area. Jax sported several cuts, but was now busy tying up the Draeken woman, while Nalea was nowhere to be seen.

"Where's Lea?" she asked to no one in particular.

"We haven't been able to find either her or Roden yet. We searched the area. It doesn't look like there were any other Draeken," one of the soldiers reported while he eyed her warily.

Her second greatest fear furrowed in her stomach. "Lea's gone." She grabbed Legian's hands. "We've got to get her back."

Numbly, Sienna looked once more at the Draeken she'd killed. She realized that killing was easy; it was the losing a bit of her soul that was the hard part.

Chapter Twenty-One

Sienna scolded herself every time she ended up in another training session with Legian. He looked like he was enjoying himself, as if these training sessions were his revenge for every time she pissed him off. *He's getting his vengeance all right*, she thought as she tied the bandana around her head to catch the sweat burning her eyes.

She couldn't see his eyes through the dark sunglasses he wore, which made it even harder to guess his moves. To make matters worse, her leg brace was still being recalibrated by Doc. And she didn't have her old brace at the cabin, leaving her to train by balancing on one leg. Serious handicap, but Legian seemed to think it was a good idea in case she was ever caught without a brace.

He lunged, and she dove to the side. He caught her ankle and she kicked back, hitting him square in the chest. He fell back, but was on his feet a split second later.

"That may work on me, but Draeken are stronger and faster. They age faster, but that does you no good in battle unless you plan to lecture them to death on English slang."

"Ha ha," she quipped.

"You can't beat them with a frontal attack. You aren't strong enough. You've got to go for their wings. They are extremely sensitive and the fastest way to take one down. You can take down a Draeken three times your size if you get hold of a wing."

"That's a bit tricky to practice, since you don't have wings," she snapped back.

He ignored her. "They protect their wings. Keep them close to their bodies. You have to find other ways to take them down, too."

"I can't do this." She let out an exasperated sigh, sat down on the floor and rubbed her bad leg.

"Yes, you can." Legian stepped closer and held out a hand.

Seizing the moment, Sienna grabbed his hand and yanked him forward as she reached for her cane. He fell, and she straddled him, pressing the cane against his neck. His eyes widened.

He smiled then he cussed. "You cheated."

"Yeah. So? I'm not the one lying on his back right now."

With a grunt in response, he brought a hand up and gingerly pushed the cane away. "I think we've had enough training for one day." He ignored her offered hand, instead pushing himself to his feet.

She smiled. "Sore loser."

"Don't think a Draeken will fall for that trick," he scolded.

"And don't think that's the only trick up my sleeve," she replied.

Inside, Jax and Ace were playing a game of gin rummy. Risa sat next to a scowling Jax. Ace was grinning.

"Let me guess. Ace is winning," Sienna said, stepping through the doorway.

"I think he's cheating," Jax said.

Ace snorted. "Poor man's down because I'm kicking his ass."

"What do you have there?" she asked, motioning to the cheese dip and nachos on the table next to Ace.

"My snack," the soldier replied without looking up. "Get your own."

She put her hands on her hips. "I don't know if you know this, but you're a guest at my home right now," she said to the man sitting on her couch.

"Doesn't mean you get my nachos."

"Fine. I'll remember that at Christmas time." She headed into the kitchen to make her own snack. She cubed the cheese and mixed in a can of diced tomatoes and peppers. As it bubbled in the microwave, she thought of Nalea. It had been three days. Apolo had been furious. He'd said that of all the trinity members, they couldn't lose Nalea to the Draeken—whatever that meant. He'd tried to check with his informant, but again received no response. It was a safe bet his cover had been blown and he was bear bait in Canada right about now. The Draeken prisoner in the basement had been even less help.

They'd sent out scouts, but they'd found nothing. It was difficult to follow a trail when there were no tracks. Everyone assumed Roden must have flown away, taking his Sephian prisoner with him and leaving them with very little to go on. Nalea's name had become taboo around the cabin. Her disappearance sat heavily, like a proverbial white elephant in the room. No one spoke of it, yet everyone was thinking about it.

Juggling her cheese and a bag of nachos in one hand and the cane in the other, Sienna hobbled back into the living room. She sat down next to Ace and crunched her chips extra loudly. When he looked at her, she smiled sweetly. "My snack. Back off."

Legian leaned forward and grabbed a couple chips. He ate them plain. Sephian food was bland, and he hadn't grown accustomed to anything spicier than Doritos yet.

Jax threw his cards down and pushed back from the table. "This is bullshit. I swear you could play Russian roulette with a fully loaded revolver and win."

Ace shrugged and leaned back in his chair. "And you like the beatings. You're a regular sub. I know what you need."

"What's that?" Jax asked.

"You need a woman to pull out the whips and chains," he replied with a wicked-ass grin.

With that, Jax barked out a laugh. "Yeah, whatever man. I'm out of here. Time for a perimeter check."

"Sure. Take out your sexual frustrations on the poor guards," Ace said.

Jax flipped his friend the bird as he stood. Risa kissed Jax, and he headed out the door, letting the screen door slam shut behind him.

Sienna sat and smiled through their banter. She needed his humor and normalcy more than she liked to admit.

Risa stretched. "I could use a nap," she mumbled through a yawn, covering her mouth.

"See you later," Sienna called out after the med-tech as she headed down the hall.

"Hold up." Ace pulled himself to his feet, the grin dropping from his face. "We gotta talk."

Risa turned, eyed him warily, and then smiled warmly. "Of course."

Ace sauntered down the hall, and the two disappeared in the guest bedroom. Sienna had set it aside for Apolo, but he'd ended up staying at the base. Jax—and therefore Risa—had claimed the open room right away to keep a close eye on Sienna, leaving everyone else in temporary shelters erected around the cabin.

She looked at Legian. "Speaking of naps, I could use one, too."

"If by nap, you mean us naked and me inside you, I'll come with you."

"No. I was thinking of that full body massage you owe me."

A scream rang out from across the hall. Sienna surged up. Legian leapt toward the door. He turned the handle and turned back to her.

"Go!" She hopped behind him.

He tore the door open and had disappeared inside before Sienna made it three steps closer. Shuffling sounds and crying emanated from the room. She pulled open the drawer to her nightstand and cursed when she remembered she'd taken that gun to the base when she first left the cabin with Legian. Slamming it shut, she hurried as quickly as her lame leg allowed. Grabbing the doorway, she stumbled into the room and froze.

Legian had a choke-hold on Ace, who was holding his gun point blank at Risa's heart.

"Jesus Christ. What's going on here?" Sienna demanded.

"Oh, thank the gods." Risa ran toward Sienna and wrapped her arms around her.

"Get away from her, traitor," Ace belted out, and Legian tightened his grip, causing the man to cough.

Sienna faced the men, still holding Risa, who was trembling. "Legian, release him."

Legian backed off slowly and Ace jumped to one side. Risa looked at him and cowered into her. "Keep him away from me," she whimpered into her neck.

Sienna patted the med-tech on the back as she eyed Ace. "What the hell happened?"

Ace opened his mouth to speak, but Risa jumped in to speak first. "He tried to seduce me. When I rejected him, he tried to rape me."

"*Bullshit*." Ace held a hand against his shoulder, a dark red stain outlining his hand. "She tried to kill me."

Risa trembled in her arms. "He's lying. I tried to protect myself. He's jealous of Jax. He said he was going to hurt me when I fought back. I swear it."

"If I wanted her dead, she'd be dead already," Ace gritted out through clenched teeth.

At that moment, Jax strolled into the room. He stopped, stared, and muttered, "What the hell's going on?"

"Jax! Gods, I'm so glad you're here." Risa ran to him and pointed at her lover's best friend. "That man tried to rape me!"

Jax looked in shock from Risa to Ace and back again. Ace said nothing, but his entire body tensed like a cable pulled too tight. Sienna prayed silently that he wouldn't snap. Then, ever so slowly, Jax's hands dropped from holding Risa. He backed away and raw anger poured over his face.

"Jax?" Risa pleaded in a whimper, reaching out to him.

"What did you do?" Jax ground out the words.

Risa's jaw dropped. "What do you mean?"

"What did she do?" he asked Ace, never taking his eyes off her.

"She tried to kill me," Ace replied. "I told her that I saw her around the video feeds the morning they went offline, and she freaked."

The video... "The letter." Sienna stared at Risa. Like a rain shower, the pieces fell into place.

"He's lying," Risa sobbed out as she backed away from Jax.

Jax scowled. "Ace never lies." He edged closer to her, his hand reaching behind his back. "And he would never, ever try to rape a woman. Anyone who knows him knows what happened to his sister." A hard look fell over him. He had made a decision. And from the way he looked at Risa, it didn't bode well for her.

In a rush, Risa charged Sienna. Sienna jumped back, stopping against the wall. Risa pulled out a blaster, and Sienna froze. There was no escape this time. Risa grabbed her arm and stepped behind her, using her as living body armor.

"Stop or else I'll kill her," Risa threatened, and the three men stopped in their tracks. "I'm sorry," she said to Jax.

"You're sorry?" Jax asked incredulously. He shook his head. "I was your perfect sap. I got you access to the officers' hall, Apolo's room…. Don't apologize for something you planned out detail by fucking detail. No. I give you kudos. You played me good. You're one hell of an actress."

Sienna could feel Risa trembling behind her. "It's not like that."

Jax glared. "Give the act up already."

"How could you, Risa? How could you betray your own people like this?" Sienna asked, trying to distract the medtech as she thought through ideas of how to get the blaster pointing at her head to be pointing at anything but her head or the men in the room.

Risa guffawed. "The Sephians aren't my people. They were never my people. The woman who gave birth to me left me to die in an alley, like I was nothing but garbage. It was a Draeken who saved me. They protected us from ourselves. And how did we show our appreciation? We stabbed them in the backs."

"You were their slaves," Sienna replied.

"No, not slaves. Not all of us. Hillas raised me as his own."

"Hillas." The single word fell from Legian's lips in no more than a whisper.

Risa turned Sienna to face Legian. "Yes, Hillas is my father. He may not be the one who impregnated my mother, but he treats me like his daughter. He is a far better father than any Sephian could be."

"He used you," Legian replied.

"No. Never."

Sienna felt the blaster nudge against her temple.

"He loves me. He didn't ask me to take this mission, but I volunteered. I did it. To protect him."

"But Hillas is dead," Sienna said.

"Hillas is not dead. But you will be."

Chapter Twenty-Two

The blaster moved against Sienna's temple as Risa adjusted her grip. Sienna seized her chance. Throwing her head back, she connected with something that made a loud crunch.

"Uh!" Risa's grip loosened, and Sienna jerked away the instant the blaster went off. Heat blasted by her face, and the smell of burnt hair filled her nostrils. In slow motion, she watched Risa aim the blaster at Jax.

Jax dove for Risa.

Risa fired.

Jax didn't stop. He chopped the med-tech in the throat, knocking her to her knees. The blaster dropped to the carpeted floor with a thud. Risa's hands clawed at her throat as she struggled for air that wouldn't come. Jax had showed Sienna that move a week ago. It was sure death, he'd said. Her windpipe had been crushed. It was just a matter of time now.

Blood poured from Risa's broken nose. Jax just stood there and stared while Risa fought to breathe. As her eyes bulged, she reached out to Jax. He did nothing as she grabbed his pant legs before sliding down into a crumpled heap on the floor.

Silence fell over the room. No one moved for what seemed like an eternity in a black hole. Finally, Jax moved forward, only to stumble. Everyone lunged forward to grab him, but Ace got there first. Sliding an arm around Jax's back, Ace helped him to the bed before sitting down on the cedar chest.

Sienna glanced toward the hall. "I'll grab a first-aid kit."

She returned from the bathroom a seconds later with her cane in hand and an armful of supplies. Legian had torn away Jax's shirt to reveal a nasty burn on his hip.

Ace continued to hold a hand against his shoulder. "You're lucky she was a bad shot. It grazed you."

Jax remained silent while he stared out the window.

Dumping the supplies on the bed, Sienna grabbed some scissors and faced Ace. He lowered his hand and fresh blood seeped through his shirt.

"Knife wound," was all he said.

"I'll call Doc, but it could take him some time to get here. In the meantime, we need to staunch the bleeding." She cut off his shirt, and then dabbed at the wound.

"It's not too deep."

She pressed a cloth against the wound, and he grimaced. "You'll need stitches."

"Nothing new to me."

And that was something she had no doubt about after seeing Ace without a shirt. Scars of all shapes and sizes littered his skin, his latest addition not making the top three for worst scars on his torso.

She stood there for a minute, keeping pressure on the wound, as she watched Legian rub salve on Jax's burn. Every now and then Jax would wince, but otherwise showed no sign of emotion.

Suddenly Ace pushed her away. "For fuck's sake, give me a needle and thread already," he muttered.

"But Doc should do that," she replied.

"I got this." He gave her a half-smile before winking.

With a wary eye, Sienna backed off and sifted through the supplies for a small pre-sealed bag labeled *Suture Kit*. She tore it open and held it out for Ace. He grabbed the bag and threaded the needle like a pro. She stared while he played doctor on his own body. "Sure I can't help?"

"Nah," he replied. His hands were steady, although his voice was tight. Stitching his own wound had to hurt like hell.

Sienna heard the screen door open, and she stepped out into the hallway to see a Sephian soldier walking into the kitchen.

"Wait up, Sana," Sienna called out to the soldier.

The Sephian woman stopped, turned, and faced her. "What can I do for you, Sienna?"

"Get Apolo and Doc up here right away. Also, on your way out, send in two able-bodied Sephians."

Sana jumped into gear quickly and without question.

Sienna stepped into the kitchen and rummaged through the cabinets. She stopped when she found what she was looking for. An old bottle of whiskey she'd bought when she wanted to kill her pain, back when she had dumbly thought booze could drown the memories of Bobby. Instead, all the stuff had done was guarantee a lousy hangover.

She carried the Texas fifth into the bedroom. She could hear water running in the bathroom. Ace came out moments later, the blood washed from his hands. His eyes lit up. "That's my kind of medicine," he said as he reached out for the bottle.

Sienna handed him the bottle and bent down to examine his new stitches. "Impressive."

"They don't call me Ace for nothing," he replied, and took a long draw before handing the bottle back to her.

Sienna stepped over to the bed where Legian had also finished patching up Jax. She offered the bottle. Without looking at her, Jax swung his legs over the side of the bed. He grunted and held his side as he dragged himself to his feet then he grabbed the bottle and stumbled out the room without even looking her in the eye. She watched him leave, and Ace jogged to catch up. He looped Jax's arm over his shoulder, and the pair disappeared down the hallway.

Adrenaline making her hands shaky, Sienna pulled together the supplies and shoved them back into the plastic pouch. She noticed the blood on her hands. Strange that she hadn't even noticed it before. The sight of it didn't bother her any longer. And that scared her. She'd changed, but she wasn't sure it was for the better.

Two Sephians stepped into the bedroom and froze when they saw the body on the floor.

Sienna pointed to the body. "Get rid of that traitor."

There were some days she wished she could get a do-over. Today would have been one of those days. Whoever had said ignorance was bliss had really nailed it. Yesterday, Risa had been one of her friends. Today, Risa had tried to kill her.

Sienna had been through a lot in the past few months, but today was the first time she truly felt she'd lost her innocence. She would never again be the trusting Sienna she used to be. She was different, jaded.

She watched without emotion as one of the men grabbed Risa's body by the shoulders and the other by her feet. They carried her out of the cabin and out of her sight. She didn't know what they would do with the body. The truth was, she didn't care. Someone she'd considered a friend had caused the deaths of hundreds of Sephians. That was unforgiveable.

Sienna walked into the bathroom and scrubbed her hands.

Even after she knew they were clean, she kept scrubbing, trying to wash away Risa's betrayal. The med-tech's actions made no sense to her. Her hand had led to the ambush, the base attack, and who knew what else. Hundreds of deaths would rest on her soul. What in the world could lead someone to do something so terrible?

Sienna didn't stop scrubbing until her hands had turned red. She turned off the water and grabbed a towel. She couldn't help feeling as though that death surrounded her, followed her. She hung the towel back on its hook and didn't realize Legian had come in until he wrapped his arms around her. She let herself relax into his embrace.

"You okay?" he asked.

"Seems like I need to redefine 'okay' every day."

He held her, saying nothing.

"I'm okay. You?" She turned around and wrapped her arms around his waist. She clung to him. With Legian, she felt safe. But safe didn't cut it. Not anymore. With a deep breath, she broke the connection. "I should check on Jax."

"Want me to come with you?"

She shook her head. "It may be better if just one of us go. How about you stay here and search through Risa's things. See if you can find out if she had anything else underway. Or, if we have any more traitors in our midst."

It took Sienna the better part of an hour to find Jax, passed out with the empty bottle of whiskey by his side. With a bit of help from a soldier on patrol, she was able to get Jax back into his bedroom, although she wasn't sure he'd appreciate the reminder once he awoke.

"Unexpected turn of events," Apolo said as she pulled a blanket up to cover Jax.

They made eye contact, and she stepped out the room, clicking the door shut behind her. Apolo followed her to the living room where Bente, Doc, and Legian waited.

"Doc, Jax has a laser burn on his hip, and Ace patched up a cut on his own shoulder. They both need to be checked," she said before she sat down next to Legian.

"As you know, I'm not skilled in human medicine, but I'll see what I can do. Where do I go?"

She nodded down the hallway, and he hustled off in that direction.

She sat there and scanned the faces in the room. Finally, she blurted out the words. "We found the traitor."

Apolo leaned forward, eyeing her with interest.

"It was Risa, the med-tech."

Murmurs filled the room.

She heard a gasp from the hallway. She looked to see Doc holding a hand to his mouth in shock. He clenched his fists, closed his eyes, and shook his head.

"Doc, Jax needs you now," Sienna called out.

The doctor jerked up. He nodded and muttered "Yes, yes," as he stumbled toward the guest room and disappeared. She had no doubt he'd blame himself—just like Jax—for not figuring Risa out earlier. She imagined there would be too much self-blame going around for a while. That's what happened when someone close betrayed you. Someone had to be blamed. And with Risa dead, people would blame themselves.

But not Sienna. She had enough stuff beating her up already. Guilt wasn't going to get added to that list. She turned back to the room and continued. "Unfortunately, we were forced to kill her before we could get much information from her. We still have no guarantees that she was operating on her own."

"What we did learn was disturbing, though," Legian added, and she turned to him. "Risa told us that Hillas lives."

The murmurs in the room turned into an uproar as the Sephians present cussed and questioned Legian.

Sienna patted the air down with her hands, trying to quiet the room. "She could have been lying, although she had no reason to lie at that point."

Apolo clenched his eyes closed for a moment before opening them. "This changes nothing. We have always suspected the Draeken tyrant survived the war. This news substantiates that suspicion. But in the past, Hillas never allowed Roden the kind of authority he's shown lately. There is something afoot in the Draeken camp."

"We'll question the prisoner." At Sienna's words, the entire room turned to her.

Apolo began pacing the floor. "We'll question Talla, sure enough. But I know that one. She won't give us anything we need." He turned on his heel when he came to the window, stopped, and faced the room. "Without my informant, we are blind. We can only hope we repaid the favor in kind today."

"Still no news yet?" Sienna asked with an optimistic raise of her eyebrows.

He shook his head. "I have to assume he is no longer viable."

"Sorry to hear that." Her words were barely above a whisper. Even though Apolo remained stoic, the news—or lack thereof—from his informant had hit him hard. Legian had told her the pair had worked together for many years. Even though he was Draeken, he was one of Apolo's closest, most trusted friends. But, because he was Draeken, Apolo would never be able to admit that to anyone. It sucked, wasn't fair, and was too much like she'd seen happen time and again on her own planet. Instead of wings, it was religion or color or some other bullshit excuse.

She leaned back into the comfort of the couch while Apolo spoke about the new alliance. Both the Americans and the Brits were on board, but she didn't think for one instant that it would be easy. Nightmares of power struggles, red tape, and deception already lurked at the outskirts of her dreams.

The next morning, after spending the entire night talking about the Draeken threat, Apolo returned to the base. Sienna was exhausted but happy. A lot had been discussed and even more had been accomplished. It had been a good night.

Jax stumbled out of the bedroom. Legian and Sienna sat on the couch, watching him as they ate breakfast. He looked like hell had frozen over as he sifted through the cabinets. After going through several cabinets, he slammed one shut, grabbed at his side with a wince, and turned to glare at her.

"Don't you have anything to fucking drink in this place?"

She handed her plate to Legian and walked into the kitchen, using her cane for support. She opened the fridge, pulled out a soda, and tossed it to Jax.

Jax ignored the can as it flew past his shoulder. His blood-shot eyes fired daggers. "That's not what I meant."

"I know exactly what you meant, and that won't fly here," she replied. "Come with me."

At first he looked like he wanted to shoot her, but then the soldier in him manned up and he followed her through the kitchen and down the stairs to the basement. The basement was small, used more as a wine cellar than anything. It had cost her a small fortune to build one in the rock-laden ground of Arkansas, and the construction company had balked at her request. But she had grown up in the Midwest and considered a basement a must-have anywhere with even a remote chance of a tornado. She'd never imagined it could double as a makeshift prison.

The Draeken prisoner sat on the floor with the black band-like material the Sephians used around her neck and wrists. The other end of the band was locked onto a steel I-beam. There was enough room in the cord for her to walk around without there being enough for her to attempt suicide. She could just reach the toilet. A basement bathroom was something Sienna had specifically requested from the construction company. And she felt completely redeemed seeing its value now, even though the guards had removed the door to keep the prisoner always in their view. The Sephians had been going to give the prisoner a bucket, which went against Sienna's morals, let alone the Geneva Conventions.

The Draeken prisoner's name was the only information she'd shared willingly, and the only thing they'd already known. Talla Kohlm didn't even look up when Sienna reached the bottom of the stairs. The Sephian guarding her, on the other hand, came to attention immediately. Sana, the consummate soldier. Way too rigid, that one.

"We won't need any more guards down here right now." At the sound of her voice, everyone in the room looked at her, including the prisoner. Sienna turned to Jax. "The prisoner is Lieutenant Jerrick's responsibility now."

Jax frowned. "I don't think this is a good idea, Sienna," he gritted out.

She stood her ground, at full height. She could feel every eye in that underground room on her. "You were there for me, and I'm here for you now, even if it doesn't feel like it. I don't care how you do it, but this prisoner is now on your shoulders. Got it?"

His eyes narrowed at her, and they stayed in the standoff for what felt like minutes before he sneered. "Yes, ma'am."

"Sana will keep an eye on the prisoner until you clean up. Get some greasy food and caffeine in you."

It was his turn to stand his ground. "No. I'm good."

"Fine. You can grab something when you assign other guards."

Without a word, he walked over to Sana, who handed him a com. She headed upstairs with a look of relief. Jax fastened the device around his throat, grabbed a folding chair, and carried it over. He opened it and sat down, his forearms resting on the seat back, and faced Talla. She sat there, glaring first at Jax then at Sienna.

Sienna held out the soda she'd grabbed before coming down. "Got this covered, Jax?"

"Covered," he muttered from his chair and took the can from her hand.

She took one last look at Talla, who was now deep in a staredown with Jax. Her wings ruffled in agitation. Sienna turned to the stairs but paused before going up the first step. "Oh, and one more thing." She waited for Jax's eyes to meet hers. "Don't kill her... yet."

Chapter Twenty-Three

Oddly, moving back to the Sephian base felt a bit like moving home. For the first time in Sienna's life, everything felt in balance. The base was now operating around the clock. Legian took over much of Apolo's role since Apolo was swamped with bureaucratic duties. After a week back on her original *human* sleep pattern, Sienna had been waking up more refreshed and energized. Several platoons, all under Major Sommers, had moved to the base, requiring many of the Sephians to bunk together to free up quarters for the soldiers. Too many changes, too many bodies in close quarters, and short tempers made most of Sienna's job schoolyard patrol.

Legian's arm lay loosely over her. She traced the mark that swirled around his forearm. "I wish we could stay like this forever."

"Someday."

Unfortunately, this wasn't *someday*. Nalea was still missing, and the shadow of the Draeken threat smothered her every thought.

Music blared from the nightstand. Startled, Sienna

grabbed her new smartphone. "Sienna speaking."

"Sienna! So good to hear your voice."

Sienna pulled the phone away and stared at it a moment before bringing it back to her ear. It had been months since she'd heard that voice. "Kat?"

"Of course it's me, sweetie. I'm back in the States, and I look forward to catching up. We must talk, Sienna. We've so much to talk about."

"Things are a bit crazy right now, but—"

"No buts, dear. I'm already in Texarkana."

Sienna ran a hand through her hair. Her mother's timing seriously sucked, but Kat was still her mother, so Sienna would make things work. "Yeah, sure. I'll pick you up at Filly's at noon. Sound good?"

"Perfect. See you soon, sweetie. Love you."

"Love you too, Kat."

Sienna sat there for a moment before setting the phone down. She nudged Legian's arm. "Wake up, sleepyhead."

He mumbled some kind of response.

"You get to meet my mother today."

His eyes jerked open, and curiosity battled with dread.

She laughed. "Don't worry. Kat's not *that* bad." She thought for a moment. "Well, yeah, she can be."

She stood and rummaged through her closet, randomly grabbing clothes. "I'll check with Sommers, and I'll have her brought in blind-folded, just like we do for press access." Over the past week, Sienna had been working with Major Sommers to establish access badges for the visitors who were bound to start checking out Earth's latest additions. Inquisitive Kat would be a great way to test security.

After throwing on a long-sleeved thermal, cargos, and hiking boots, Sienna grabbed her cane, left Legian, and hobbled straight to the Commons to grab breakfast. Fresh muffins sat cooling on the counter. She ate one as she watched the sunrise on one of the digital screens brought in for the humans' benefit. Warm blueberries burst like hot caviar bubbles in her mouth. After licking her fingers clean, she washed down the muffin with a glass of orange juice.

She then grabbed a couple muffins and a carton of juice before looking at her cane. Setting it back down, she took a wicker basket full of fruit and dumped the contents. Adding back in a couple of bananas along with the muffins and orange juice, she walked clumsily down the hallway to the holding cells, carrying the basket in one hand while gripping her cane in the other.

When she reached the only inhabited cell, Talla looked at her. Her wings, covered in the usual Draeken tattoos, hung loosely out from her sides. Her long, silver hair was fastened on top of her head. She looked exhausted, no doubt from the daily rounds of unending interrogation. A small part inside Sienna was glad to see that the prisoner had survived Jax's sour mood. Sienna hadn't been confident she would survive a night, let alone a month.

Even though Jax now had guards assigned to his prisoner, he still spent hours every day overseeing her "care".

"Here." She held out a muffin first to Jax and the other guard before offering one to Talla.

Jax didn't move an inch. "No thanks. Already ate." He sat with the folding chair turned around and leaned forward on the backrest, keeping his prisoner under close scrutiny.

Talla snatched the muffin from Sienna's hand and sat facing away from Jax to eat it. He watched the prisoner while she ate and ignored him.

Sienna almost grinned when Jax narrowed his eyes and gave her the classic Jax scowl. Yeah, Jax was back. "Can I get you anything else?" she asked, setting the basket on the floor next to his chair.

"Nah. We're good," Jax replied.

"You know, Talla, things would go easier if you were willing to meet us halfway," Sienna said.

The Draeken glared at Sienna before giving them her back once again.

"Have it your way, then. You and Jax have fun. Oh, and Talla…" Sienna waited for the Draeken to straighten. "You better rest up. You're scheduled for another round of interrogation today." With that, Sienna left the holding cells.

She was surprised to find Apolo waiting for her outside the door, peeling an orange. He held out an arm. Sienna took it, and he walked her into his old quarters, which had been converted into briefing rooms. She sat on the newly-added leather couch while he took an overstuffed chair across from her.

"I wanted to stop by before I leave for England tonight," he said before popping a slice of orange in his mouth.

Her brow furrowed. "You're leaving already? I thought it would take longer for them to prepare for your arrival."

"I did, too. Evidently the Brits are quite excited to get their hands on our technology."

Sienna nodded in silent agreement. *I bet they are.*

He smiled. "They are also quite accommodating. They've established an old wartime bunker for us. Sunlight-free."

"That's the British for you. I'm guessing you'll acquire an addiction to fine teas and crumpets in no time," Sienna said with a smile. "With my luck, the Americans will try to relocate our U. S. group to an army base where we can be monitored twenty-four/seven."

His lips thinned. "Make no mistake, we are already being monitored. Every second of every minute of every day." He glanced down the hallway. "Tell me, how does Jax fare?"

Sienna raised her eyebrows. "He's going to be fine. Doc says his burn is healing nicely."

"I'm not talking about his injury."

She leaned back into the couch. "Risa's betrayal knocked him down for a bit." *It knocked us all down.* "But he's getting right back on. I've assigned him to our Draeken prisoner to keep him busy. He's been quite diligent in his duties."

Apolo smiled. "It was wise to assign him to the prisoner. I think it was exactly what the soldier in him needed."

Sienna shrugged. "I figured only drunkenness or duty would work with him, and duty seemed like a healthier plan. Everything would be easier if only Nalea was back." Sienna winced, regretting saying those last words.

Apolo inhaled deeply. "Roden has her, and he's keeping her alive for a reason. There is hope. However, having a complete trinity is a critical strength of a leader. Being without one is a weakness in the eyes of the Sephians."

"But replacing Nalea would also be a sign of weakness," Sienna said. "It would show that you're giving up on her."

Apolo said, "And that, to me, that is unacceptable."

They sat in silence for several moments while Apolo finished the orange and Sienna stared at the wall.

"We will make it our priority to find Nalea, and I will work with the Brits on this as well. She is crucial."

"How so?"

He mused for a moment. "That is something she needs to tell you herself. What I know, I know in confidence. All I can say is, the longer the Draeken have her, the greater the risk."

Sienna eyed him strangely, but he said nothing more. "I wonder if Roden knows."

Apolo jerked. "Why do you think that?"

Sienna shrugged. "I don't know exactly. But, there was something off about the meeting that day. It was almost as though Roden had planned all along to take Nalea. He seemed awfully focused on her."

"Perhaps Roden suspects something. All the more reason to search for her and stop Roden."

"Lieutenant-Colonel Jerrick has offered to help out with the search," Sienna said. "Let's hope he meant it."

"Time will tell. The Americans have shown strong initial support."

"By support, you mean the troops he's assigned to the base?" Sienna shook her head. "They're here to keep an eye on us, not to keep the Draeken out." She rested her head on the back of the couch as she stared up at the ceiling for a long moment before turning back to Apolo. "We have a long road ahead of us, don't we?"

Apolo smiled weakly. "While our alliance isn't yet written in stone, we're all on the same page when it comes to the Draeken. We'll have to build from that." He stood and looked around. "I'm short on time. I should be going. I'll give you my location and will set up communications once I'm settled in there. Even though our British hosts have offered a full telecommunications setup, I also desire something a little less *privy* to eager ears."

"Good luck. And, Apolo? Thank you. I treasure both your leadership and our friendship."

"As do I." With that, he gave her a formal Sephian hand-shake then turned and walked out the door without another word.

Sienna headed outside to wait for her mother's transport ship to land. Instead of standing idly around, she spent the time walking the perimeter, stopping at every checkpoint to chat with the Sephians, who looked to her in order to learn about humans.

As the ship touched down with her mother inside, Sienna leaned against the wall. At some point during the past several months, she realized that she considered the Sephians more her people than humans. The Sephians were her people, and she'd do anything for them. The idea didn't disturb her. Instead, it made her proud.

Chapter Twenty-Four

"Are we good here?" Sienna asked.

"All scans came through clean. Your visitor is cleared for access," Quincy replied as he reached to remove her visitor's blindfold.

Her mother looked just like she had the day Sienna had seen her last, except her brown hair with striking waves of gray was shorter now. Kat had always been attractive, and age hadn't changed that one bit.

Kat rubbed her eyes, looked around, and then threw out her arms when she found her daughter. "Sienna!"

Sienna smiled, only to be pulled into a full hug. "Sorry about not being there to pick you up. I got a bit tied up here."

"It's okay. I've missed you so much, sweetie." Her mother pulled back to take in her surroundings. "This is unbelievable, Sienna," she said motioning around the hangar. "And you're in the middle of all this."

"C'mon." Sienna motioned to her mother. "I'll show you the gardens."

Kat frowned, bringing out the fine lines at her eyes. "Can

I have a tour? I was hoping to see the rooms where all the technology is, like for communications."

"Only the gardens are approved for guests. I'll see if I can get you more clearance next time."

Kat smile flattened in disappointment. "All right then. To the gardens."

"They're really something. You'll see."

As they went down a level toward the gardens, they walked past several guards—both human and Sephian, though few of the interracial teams spoke to each other. The Sephians towered above the humans by several inches. Unlike humans, Sephian females stood as tall as their male counterparts. That genetic trait did nothing to help average-height Sicnna earn respect. Her size and her inability to pull energy to heal only made the Sephians believe humans were all the more fragile.

As the human face of the Sephian force, the soldiers came to her—or Jax—rather than going to any Sephian, and she doubted it had much to do with her authority. Racism was still running rampant across the base—on both sides—something she hoped would fade over time. At least they both saw the Draeken as a common threat.

"...I thought."

Sienna glanced over at Kat. "Sorry. What'd you say?"

"Still the daydreamer, I see." Kat smiled. "I was saying that this place is more normal than I'd expect. I don't know what I thought I'd see, but this,"—Kat motioned around her —"isn't much different than any military base."

Sienna shrugged. "Guess other than a few trillion or so miles separating our people, we're not that different from each other." Although there would always be some biological differences. They had brightened the lights when the troops came. Now the Sephians needed to wear sunglasses all the time, but it was a small price considering the alternative.

With a *swoosh*, the door to the gardens opened, and Kat sucked in a breath. "Oh my. Incredible."

"These gardens provide all the food for the Sephians on this base." While the gardens that spanned over an acre were an incredible sight, Sienna had been here long enough to notice that the plants were quickly growing more and more sparse. The knot in her stomach continued to grow.

The gardens weren't intended to provide sustenance while on-world. While the Sephians were slowly accustoming their biology to Earth foods, they would be hard-pressed to support themselves without the gardens—and the gardens couldn't last much longer. The Sephians needed to adapt fast, but having the proverbial Draeken wolf at the door didn't make things any easier.

They took a seat on a bench under a fruit tree. The air was heavier here. The Sephian home world's atmosphere had slightly higher concentrations of oxygen, and while the Sephians handled Earth's air just fine, their plants were more sensitive.

Kat sighed. "Oh, Sienna. I wish you weren't entangled in this mess."

Sienna frowned. "I thought coming face to face with life beyond Earth was your greatest dream."

"It was, but that was before you were pulled into this. But don't you worry, dear. I'm going to make everything better."

"What are you talking about?"

Her mother came to her feet and pulled something out of her purse.

"Kat?"

She made no response as she lay what looked like a piece of black plastic wrap over a control panel. Instantly it melted around the panel and started to grow.

Sienna's frozen as she stared at the growing black liquid.

Kat tugged Sienna's hand. "Come. It's finished. We must hurry."

Sienna yanked out of Kat's grip and stepped back. "What have you done?" She scrambled in her pocket, found the comm she always carried, and hit the panic button, which would now be sending a constant signal to both the tech-hub as well as Legian.

"I did what needed to be done, dear. The Sephians are here to commit genocide. Life beyond Earth is still my greatest dream. *All* life." Kat unbuttoned her sleeve and pulled up her shirt, revealing a tattoo of the Draeken imperial family's symbol.

Sienna brought a hand up to cover her mouth. "Oh, Kat, you didn't."

Her mother smiled as she glanced down at the tattoo then her smile fell, and she snapped at her daughter. "We must hurry. We don't have long. We must get out of here before it's too late."

"*Mom,*" Sienna snapped. "These are my people. I'm never leaving them."

Kat's lips thinned. "I'm sorry it has to be this way. But I won't sit by and watch the genocide of an entire race. Good bye, Sienna." She turned to run, but Sienna tackled her.

"Sienna, no! You'll kill us both!" she cried out from under her daughter.

"Then deactivate that thing."

Kat looked confused. "I can't."

Footsteps pounded the floor, sending vibrations through her. She looked up to find the soldiers first on the scene.

She pointed to growing black liquid-like substance and yelled out, "She's attempting to sabotage the base!"

They looked at the substance and back to Sienna as if waiting for instruction. The door to her other side opened, and she watched Legian, shirtless and barefoot, lead in several Sephian troops. *Oh, thank God.*

Everything felt slow-motion as he took in Sienna, Kat, and then finally the black substance. The look on his face was pure dread.

Legian's eyebrows shot up as he faced Sienna. "Find cover! The bomb is small enough that we may be able to burn it in time." He visibly swallowed. "If it burns," he said quieter, clearly just to Sienna. "The blast will still be powerful enough to destroy this room."

And everyone in it. The terror emanating from every Sephian present was answer enough. As he lifted his gun, she wished she had her weapon, but protocol prevented her from carrying a weapon when with a visitor. "Get down!" she shouted to the human troops. But none listened. Instead, they pulled out their weapons as well, following suit with Legian.

She pushed her mother against the floor hard, and fortunately the woman didn't push back. Armageddon broke out when the Sephians opened blaster fire above Sienna.

The air grew hot as the weapons continued to fire for several long seconds. Sienna closed her eyes and pressed her head into her mother's back, who was shouting out accusations against the Sephians. *She'd been too late. The bomb had grown too much—*

The explosion sent Sienna flying off Kat and through the air. She crashed into a bench, knocking her breath from her lungs. Fire burned her skin, and she sucked in a breath.

Eyes, nose...

Throat...

No, her lungs were on fire.

She couldn't breathe.

Blackness.

Sienna came awake with a moan scratching her raw throat. Trying to open her burned eyes, tears began to pour against the cold air. All she saw was the large Sephian holding her, golden tears streaming down his darkened face.

She wanted to tell him how good it was to see him, how she knew he'd survive. But she settled for "Hey".

Much of her body hurt, like she'd been out in the sun all day and was now the center attraction in a dodgeball tournament. She frowned, or at least tried to. Strangely, some parts of her were completely numb. She glanced down at her blistered hands. They weren't numb, but her shoulder—and much of her face—felt *weird*. "Help me up."

"You're in shock. I need to get you to the med-hub." She hadn't heard that level of concern in Legian's voice since the base attack.

"I'll be okay," she replied, trying to pull herself up but finding no strength to do so.

Reluctantly, Legian pulled Sienna up, holding her carefully. She glanced around. Most of the human troops were spread across the floor, motionless, many clearly never getting up again. Several of the Sephians were down as well, but the med-techs were already helping them. From the look of Legian's skin, he'd gone through several donors while she was out. Then she spotted her mother sitting in the middle of the mess, her hair gone and blisters covering her face.

"How many people did you kill today?"

Her mother made no response.

"You betrayed the Sephians, the United States, and your own daughter," she said, coughing between words.

"I told you, Sienna. I couldn't stand for genocide. The Sephians want to wipe out an entire race."

"It's not like that. They're here to protect us."

Kat looked up. "I love you, Sienna, but your friends have blinded you. I never wanted to hurt you."

"I know, Kat. I wish to God you didn't do this. Don't you realize that Sephian law has no gray area when it comes to treason?" she asked softly. She felt like her heart was in a vise. She took in a breath, though it burned to do so. "Katherine Wolfe, you are a traitor. And by Sephian law, the penalty for treason is immediate execution."

Sienna glanced up at Legian. His lips tightened. She wanted him to do it, but she knew that she needed to do it. Kat was Sienna's responsibility and no one else's. Yet, the thought was unbearable. She nodded as much as her stressed muscles would allow.He handed her his blaster.

Sienna lifted it, the weight causing it to wobble in her hand, but she was close enough that aim didn't matter.

A sad look of acceptance came over Kat's face. She held out her arms. "I love you."

"I love you, too," Sienna said.

Then she squeezed the trigger.

Chapter Twenty-Five

S ienna never cried.

She'd made sure Kat received a proper burial. Despite her last actions in life, her mother had helped out many people as a humanitarian. Kat had always been her mentor, teaching her the hard lessons of life. And it seemed she'd had one lesson left.

Being a leader means you have to make the hardest sacrifices.

She didn't hate her mother. She couldn't. With her hands braced on the sink, Sienna stared at her reflection in the mirror. The left side of her face was scabbed, with no hope of healing without massive scarring. She'd surprised everyone by not dying. With third degree burns over a third of her body, that she hadn't succumbed to infection was a miracle thanks to Sephian medicine.

Once she healed enough, she'd shave off what was left of her hair. In the meantime, she didn't care what she looked like. She had more important things to worry about.

Like ensuring the Sephians a safe future on Earth.

Pushing off from the sink, Sienna started her slow inspection of the base. She knew where to find Jax at least; at this same time every day, he'd be in the holding cell watching their Draeken prisoner.

Finally, long after sunset, she went back to her room and read for a while. She didn't know how long she stayed up, but she knew she'd been asleep for hours when Legian stepped into the room. She awoke at the sound of his footsteps. The book lay across her chest, still open to the page she last read. She set it on the nightstand and watched him walk over to the bed.

"You're home." She muffled a yawn and made room for him in the bed.

"Home," he murmured as he sat down on the mattress and gave her a soft kiss. "I like the sound of that."

She leaned into him and drifted away, letting the Draeken threat wait until tomorrow.

END OF BOOK 1

Continue on to Book 2, *Implosion*, today!

Available Now

IMPLOSION

Part Two of the Colliding Worlds Trilogy

Desperate times call for desperate schemes . . .

The gold-skinned Sephians have reached a precarious peace with humans in their efforts to drive the winged Draeken from Earth . As human-Sephian forces peck at the Draeken defenses, we soon learn that things are never as simple as right and wrong, good versus evil.

Sephian warrior Nalea exists only to kill Draeken, and she's good at her job. But when she's captured by Roden Zyll, a high-ranking Draeken commander, she discovers a chance at ending a decades-long war. Only one problem: she has to work with her most hated enemy.

As the two enemies plan a coup, they must play both sides, guiding each of their people deeper into the bloody feud. If the coup is successful, peace is possible. If they fail, every Earth nation will be yanked into a war that no one has a chance of winning.

Get your copy today!

Also by Rachel Aukes

Fringe Series

Fringe Runner

Fringe Station

Fringe Campaign

Fringe War

Fringe Legacy

Colliding Worlds Trilogy

Collision

Implosion

Explosion

The Deadland Saga

100 Days in Deadland

Deadland's Harvest

Deadland Rising

The Tidy Guides Series (Nonfiction)

The Tidy Guide to Writing a Novel

The Tidy Guide to Self-Editing Your Novel

Standalone Fiction

Stealing Fate

About the Author

Rachel Aukes is the award-winning author of *100 Days in Deadland*, which made Suspense Magazine's Best of the Year list. She is also a Wattpad Star, her stories having over five million reads. When not writing, she can be found flying old airplanes across the Midwest countryside and catering to an exceptionally spoiled fifty-pound lapdog.

Join Rachel's spam-free readers club to hear about new releases: www.rachelaukes.com/newsletter

Acknowledgments

With many thanks to Laurel Kriegler and Terri King for making my stuff look good; to my beta readers Rob Shores and Kay Smillie for catching the stuff that could cause big problems; to Brian for the hugs; to Ellie for the endless supply of doggie kisses; and to *you* for picking up this story and opening the worlds within it.

www.ingramcontent.com/pod-product-compliance
Lightning Source LLC
Chambersburg PA
CBHW071409100726
47908CB00004B/1117